A COWBOY'S PROMISE

Cowboy Dreamin' 9

I0520180

Sandy Sullivan

Erotic Romance

Erotic Romance

A Cowboy's Promise
Copyright © 2016 Sandy Sullivan
E-book ISBN: 978-1-944122-24-9

First E-book Publication: April 2016
First Print Publication: April 2016

Cover design by Dawné Dominique
Edited by Stephanie Balistreri
Proofread by Ariana Gaynor
All cover art and logo copyright © 2016 by Sandy Sullivan

Dedication

I am sad to see this series end, but I know the Young brothers have all found their happily ever after and that makes me happy. Each and every one of these boys holds a special place in my heart and I hope you all have enjoyed reading their stories as much as I have writing them.
Stay tuned!
There may be 1 more in the wings!

A Cowboy's Promise
Cowboy Dreamin' 9

Sandy Sullivan

Chapter One

"I'm gonna shoot your ass, Joseph Young! Don't you come around Jessie no more! You hear me."

Joey ran across the field toward his truck in his bare feet, hopping every couple of steps when he stepped on a rock. *Damn it!* His shirt hung down his back, covering the top of his naked ass as his belt buckle clinked every few steps. He carried his boots and his cowboy hat in one hand while he tried to get in his pants pocket for his keys with the other.

Ping. Ping.

Buckshot hit the back of his tailgate. "Crazy fuckin' old man."

Ping. Ping.

"I'm leavin', damn it! Quit shootin' at me!"

"Get your ass off my property. If you show up here again, this won't be buckshot, boy."

"Stop it, Daddy!" Jessica Marshall yelled from the front porch.

"Get back in the house, Jessica."

"Joey? Are you all right?"

He could see her standing in her bare feet, jeans, and a tank top.

Boy, she'd dressed fast after her father caught them in her room in a state of semi-undress. "I'm fine. Go on in the house, Jess. I'll see you later."

"No you won't!"

Ping. Ping.

"Daddy, quit shooting at him."

"I'll teach his ass to come sniffing around my baby girl."

"I'm a grown woman. Stop acting like a fool."

"You're still my baby. You won't be hookin' up with one of them Young boys. They're all just lookin' to get in bed with a young lady like you, Jess. Think about it."

"I have, Daddy. This is crazy. Joey isn't like that."

"I know boys. They're all the same."

Ping. Ping.

He ducked as he reached the side of his truck, fumbling with the latch on the door. *Duh, locked.* Once he finally got his keys in his hands, he unlocked the door, and tossed the things he had in his hand inside the cab.

He had to admit, the one thing he wanted from her was her body when this whole thing started, but he'd thought about her a lot lately and he really liked Jessica. Her daddy was probably right though. He didn't have a lot to offer a woman. He worked on his parent's ranch with the horses, caring for them, breaking them and occasionally riding a few bucking broncs when there was a rodeo close enough to San Antonio.

A drink sounded good right about now after the evening had left him with blue balls. Maybe he'd head home to see if one of his brothers would go into town to The Dusty Boot for a beer. It was early, right?

Every one of his brothers now had a woman of their own. He wouldn't be finding any of them ready to go out for the night. It sucked being the baby of the family even at his age.

That didn't make him too old for Jessica, right? Twenty-two to thirty-one wasn't a bad spread even if he'd had an eye on her since she was sixteen. She was legal and he aimed to take advantage of the fact even if her daddy didn't like him much.

He drove up to the gates of Thunder Ridge, punching in the code to open the gates. It appeared the group was having a bonfire outside the main lodge of the guest ranch he helped run with his family—all nine, plus these days eight of his brothers had found either wives or girlfriends in the last couple of years.

As for himself, he wasn't ready to settle down. Not yet. Not him. All of his older brothers had, but he was having too much fun being the bachelor he was.

Once he drove up to the house, he shut off his truck and wiggled around so he could make himself presentable. Luckily, it wasn't far from Jessica's to his parent's place, but he still drove without his boots so now he had to put them back on his feet.

Tap, tap, tap. He jerked his head around to find his mother standing next to the truck, staring hard at him through the window.

"What are you up to, young man?" his mother asked with a raised eyebrow. Even in her mid-sixties, she was a beautiful woman with her long dark hair pulled back in a braid down her back, straw cowboy hat adorning her head, and her brown eyes sparkling in mischief.

"Nothing, Mom."

"Why are you getting dressed in your truck? Were you over bugging Jessica again?"

"I was at her place, yeah."

"It appears her daddy didn't like you sniffin' around his daughter. Your truck is full of dings."

"I know," he said, pushing open the door. He'd have to check his truck when he could see better. "Where is everyone?" With a slam, he shut the door so he could face his mother.

She pointed behind her. "Down by the bonfire. Most of them are enjoying a nice evening with the guests."

"Are you loosening up your 'no messin' with the guests' policy, because I'm sure I could find me a pretty lady down there."

Her hands on her hips stance made him feel like a kid again, like when he'd got into trouble and got grounded for it.

"No, but I can't very well enforce it when you don't seem to care what I say about it."

He shoved his hands in his pockets as he rocked back on the heels of his boots. "I care, Mom. It's just when the women come onto me, it's real hard to resist."

"I'm sure it is." She tapped the brim of his cowboy hat. "Go on."

"Thanks. I'm gonna see if any of them will go into town with me and shoot some pool or somethin'. It's too early to turn in."

"One of them might. Take Chris, that young wrangler we just hired." She leaned in on her tiptoes to kiss his cheek. Even though she wasn't short, by any means, all of the boys towered over her by several inches. "You boys be careful."

"We will."

He finished tucking in his shirt as he approached the fire where several guests sat around talking to each other, while his brothers chimed in every once in a while with a remark. Chris sat on one of the benches between two pretty girls he'd seen check-in the day before. Joey rolled his eyes. "Chris!"

"What?" the new kid yelled back without taking his gaze off the pretty brunette next to him.

"Let's go to town."

"Why?"

"I need a drink," Joey said, stopping directly in front of Chris and the two women.

"Take one of your brothers. I'm off work."

"No, you. Come on."

Chris's gaze shifted to land on him. "Fine." He stood, bowing to the two women. "I'll see you ladies tomorrow on the ride at nine in the mornin'."

"We can't wait." The blonde grinned a nice pearly white smile. "Have fun."

"Oh, we will." Joey grabbed his arm. "I'll drive."

As they headed back to his truck, Chris said, "We could have taken them with us, you know."

"They're guests. You know my mom's rule about messin' with the guests."

"Yeah, but it's not like I'm going to sleep with either of them. I was talking to them, that's all." Chris popped open the passenger side door and slid inside. "I thought you were over at Jessica Marshall's house?"

"I was until her daddy caught us."

"Well that blows."

"Yeah." Joey started the truck and backed out of the spot before he headed down the long driveway back toward the front gates of the guest ranch. The wrought iron blocking the road coming onto the ranch slid open to allow them to drive out.

"What are you gonna do now?"

"I don't know. I like her, but a piece of ass ain't worth gettin' shot at."

"He shot at you?"

"With buckshot, yeah. Good thing he didn't hit me, but I'm sure my truck looks like shit now."

"You need to find a girl who will be an occasional roll between the sheets. You're too young to worry about settlin' down."

"Who said anything about settlin' down? All I wanted from her was a good lay." He pushed his hat back on his head. "I don't know. There's somethin' about her. I mean she pretty, got a nice rack, kisses like she ain't no virgin, yet when we were together tonight, she seemed shy. Like she didn't know the first thing about havin' sex."

"She's barely twenty-two, man. Find yourself a lady who knows how to treat a man."

"I guess."

"Trust me, bro. I bet you can find some pretty thing at the bar."

"I certainly have a case of blue balls right now."

"Been that long?"

"A few months, yeah." He glanced over at his friend and then back to the road. "What about you?"

"I could get laid. It's been a while for me too." Chris tapped his fingers on his thigh for a moment. "There are some pretty women at the bar, but maybe it's not such a good idea to hook up with one for one night."

"Yet you want me to?" Joey asked as they drove down the main street of Bandera.

The Dusty Boot sat to the right of the street with several trucks in various makes and models, in their parking lot. The sign above the western motif of the building depicted a boot with a spur dangling from the back. It was the Young brothers' home away from home on any given night of the week. The place looked busy for a Tuesday night. *Good. I need to unwind.*

"Sure. It's right up your alley, Joey. Find some hot babe, get your rocks off, and then worry about your future."

Once he found a parking spot next to the dumpster, they both crawled out of his truck, slamming the doors with a bang.

Music from the bar flowed through the doors as people moved in and out. Joey really liked the band they had here. They were pretty talented. They'd even played a barbeque

Paige's family had put on at their church a couple of years ago.

Summer tourist season was upon them now, which made the ranch busier than ever. More and more people came to their ranch every summer and this one was no exception. His mother said the other day, they were booked solid for this month, with a waiting list for some weekends. Not that he minded. The business of keeping the horses everyday made for a demanding job since he was in charge of the animals—breaking, feeding, trail rides and the like. There was also a rodeo this weekend in San Antonio he wanted to do. He got his adrenaline rush from riding bucking horses. He didn't do too bad at it either.

Chris slapped him on the back as they walk through the double doors of the building. *Man, the place* is *crowded tonight.* He glanced around for a place to sit, noting two stools at the far end of the bar. "Let's go."

His friend brought up the rear as they made their way through the crowd hoping the stools would be there when they finally finished bobbing and weaving amongst the tight pack of bodies. Rhinestones and tight jeans in the sea of cowboy hats seemed to be the flavor of the evening. He knew it had been a good idea to come here.

They got to the two seats, taking the ones at the end of the bar. Lily Richards was serving this end of the group. He really did think she was kind of pretty with her black hair brushing the edge of her waist as the thick braid fell down her back. Unfortunately, for him, she wasn't his type. He wasn't into the kind of woman who tended bar. Give him a nice little cowgirl and he'd be happy as a pig in shit.

"Whatcha drinkin', boys?" Lily asked stopping in front of them.

"Couple of beers, please," Chris answered. "How's it hanging, Lily?"

"Just fine, Chris. Busier than a bull during matin' season here tonight, but then again, it's always busy here during the summer." She poured two beers and set them down in front of them. "You boys hanging out tonight?"

"Yeah. Joey got his ass shot at by old man Marshall so we're hookin' him up."

"Shut up, Chris."

Lily laughed. "Why am I not surprised by that statement?" She tapped the bar with her knuckle. "I'll check on you two in a bit. If you need another, holler."

Joey turned on the stool to take in the crowd around them. He recognized several women in a group near the back. A few he'd even been with. One waved. He tipped his hat. She excused herself from the group to head in their direction. "Ah, shit."

"What?" Chris asked as he spun around.

"She's comin' over here."

Chris laughed. "You asked for it, I'm sure."

"I was bein' friendly."

"A little too friendly."

"Hi, Joey."

"Jennifer."

"You here alone?" she asked, looking from side to side.

"No. I'm here with Chris."

"You know what I mean. You gotta a girl with you?" She stepped close enough to brush her thigh against his knee.

"Nope."

Chris elbowed him.

"I mean yeah." He noticed a pretty little thing nursing a glass of wine next to him. "I'm with her."

Joey placed his hand on the woman's shoulder. When she looked up at him, he was startled to realize he knew her from somewhere, although he couldn't place her at the moment. "Hey, babe. Do you need another glass of wine?"

"Uh, no."

"How about a dance?"

"Uh, no. I'm here to unwind, nothing more."

He turned his stool to face her. "Since we came together, I figure we should dance or something."

The woman glanced over his shoulder at Jennifer, and then met his gaze again. He tried communicating to her what he wanted. Her eyes widened when he shifted his gaze from her to Jennifer and back.

"Oh, of course. Let me finish my glass and we'll dance."

"Sure, honey."

He swung back toward Jennifer for a moment. Her eyes had become slits of indignation before she turned on her heels and stomped back toward the group at the back table. When he faced the woman sitting next to him at the bar again, he said, "Thank you for going along with me."

She took a sip of her drink. "Not someone you wanted to hang with tonight?"

"Not really. I dated her several months ago and she got real possessive."

"Ah."

He held out his hand for her to shake. "My name is Joseph Young."

"Nice to meet you, Joseph. I'm Clarissa."

"I am assuming you are here alone?"

"Yes, but as I said, I'm only here to unwind from work before I go home—alone."

He nodded and smiled. "I understand. So what do you do, Clarissa, that you need to unwind from?"

"I'm a trauma nurse."

"Wow. That must be really hard."

"It is. Some days it's very rewarding, but other days, it's very difficult to separate yourself from all the hurt, death, and crap that people do to themselves and to others." She took another sip of her wine and placed the glass back on the bar. "Tonight, I need the noisy atmosphere of this bar to take my mind off of what I saw today."

"I'm sorry to hear that."

She shrugged as she flashed him a little smile. "It's okay." She looked across the bar, and then back at him. "What are you drinking?"

"Just beer."

"Cowboy's choice of beverages, huh?"

"Yeah." He smiled as he reached out and touched her bare arm. "It's a guy thing."

She glanced down to where he touched her and then back up at him. "Sorry, Joey, but I'm not looking for a hook up. I have a boyfriend."

He removed his hand as he nodded in understanding. "Hands off. Got it."

"I don't mind sitting here shooting the shit with you though, that is unless you were really here to pick someone up for the night."

"Not really." He looked over her shoulder for a second. "Well, yeah, kind of. I had a problem with an old man, a shot gun, and his twenty-two-year-old daughter earlier. I've got a good case of blue balls, right now."

She tossed back her head and laughed. The sound was cute. A little snort and a giggle was the only way he could describe it. "Poor baby."

"I know. It's terrible, right?"

"Yes, yes it is, but I'm sure you will survive."

"I don't know. There's this nurse I know, who kind of put me off. She wouldn't treat my injury."

A grin played on her lips as she shook her head. "This nurse knows you won't die from a case of blue balls."

"I don't know. It's awful painful."

"I'm sure it is."

He took a drag off his beer, swallowing the malty liquid in a cool wash of goodness running down his throat. Yeah, beer was definitely a guy thing, although he knew lots of women who drank beer. "So, are you from around here?"

"Not really. I moved to the area a few years back."

"Do you live in Bandera?"

"Yeah. I work in San Antonio at one of the hospitals, but I rent a small house here. I like the quiet. San Antonio is very noisy. I do the craziness at the hospital. This gives me the quiet to contemplate things." She brought her glass of wine to her lips to take a long drink. "What about you?"

"My family owns a guest ranch a few miles outside of town. I help run things there with my eight brothers and their wives."

"Eight brothers? Holy shit. Your mom must have been one busy woman."

"Yes, she was and still is. It's great to have a big family."

"Where are you in the pecking order?"

"The youngest."

She tilted her head to the side and smiled. "Ah, the baby of the family."

One shoulder lifted in a shrug. "I guess."

"What do you do on the ranch?"

"I'm the head wrangler. I handle the horses for the guests to ride, break new ones we buy, and that kind of thing."

"A real cowboy then."

"As real as they come."

She glanced down to the floor. "So those dusty boots are for real."

"Yep."

"Nice."

"Where is your family?"

"Back east. Philadelphia to be exact."

"You moved here from Pennsylvania?"

"Yes. I like Texas. I love the weather and I love the animals. There just wasn't enough space for me back East. I needed room to stretch out."

"Texas has that for sure."

Her glass sat empty on the bar. "Do you want another? I'm buying since you saved me."

"No, thank you. I really need to get home. My boyfriend will be wondering where I am since it's going on ten now and I'm usually home by eight-thirty. I'm surprised he hasn't called my cell yet."

"He sounds kind of possessive."

"Sometimes, yes, but only in the best way." She gave him a wink and got to her feet.

"Thank you for the chat, Joseph. You seem like a really nice guy. I hope you have some luck tonight and manage to take care of your problem."

"Thank you for helping me out, Clarissa. I hope to see you again soon."

"See you around."

He tipped his hat as she moved around him and headed for the door.

The rest of the night he managed to keep himself away from the overzealous women of Bandera. He probably shouldn't have since the point to being here was to get laid, but after talking with Clarissa, he realized not everything came down to getting your rocks off. Chris managed to find a woman and disappeared right before closing time. He figured his friend and fellow ranch worker could find his own way home.

Joey crawled into his truck about two a.m., turned the key and headed back for Thunder Ridge.

Friday night had been a bust for him all the way around. Nothing seemed to have worked in his favor, not Jessica, and certainly not Clarissa. Oh well. It wasn't like he hadn't been in this situation before or wouldn't be in it again before his bachelor days were through.

Tomorrow would come with the rising of the sun. Work would be his top priority since he needed to get to the feed store by the end of the day to get some supplies for the horses. They'd run low on grain this week and he figured he'd hit Milligan's after the rush in the afternoon. Most local ranchers did their shopping first thing in the morning. His parents wouldn't mind if he slept in a little since he didn't have first ride outs and that little buckskin mare he'd purchased last weekend needed to be worked.

Headlights came at him from the direction of home. He wondered who in the hell was out headed for town at this time of the night. Probably one of his brothers on a middle of the night pregnancy craving run. Callie and Candace were both expecting in the coming months. That's one thing he wasn't looking forward to once he did decide to settle down with one girl, the craziness of having kids. He liked kids, sure, but they were a lot of work, and he just didn't have that itch right now.

The vehicle slowed as they met in the roadway.

When the driver's side window went down, he wasn't surprised to see Jeremiah at the wheel.

"Headed out for a midnight snack?"

Jeremiah rolled his eyes. "Yeah. Callie woke up with a craving for moose tracks ice cream. We don't have any at the house so I'm headed into town to see if the local corner market is open and has some, otherwise, I'll be driving into San Antonio."

"That sucks."

"Oh well. It's my life for the moment. She won't be pregnant forever, thank goodness." He tipped his chin like guys always do. "Coming back from The Dusty Boot?"

"Yep."

"Alone?"

"Yep."

"Rough night?"

"Yep."

"You are full of answers tonight."

"Nothing to tell."

"I heard you got shot at my Jessica Marshall's old man earlier."

"Mom has a big mouth."

"Get caught with your pants down?"

He shook his head and smiled a little. "You could say that."

"You really need to stay away from that girl. Her dad is crazy."

"Don't I know it."

Jeremiah's cell phone jingled. "I better go. I'll see you tomorrow."

"I'll be around."

"Be careful, there were several deer on the side of the road up ahead."

"Thanks."

"Later." He heard Jeremiah pick up the call just as he was driving away. "Yes, baby. I'll be home as soon as I can. I might have to go into San Antonio."

Joey laughed at how pussy-whipped his brother was by his wife. Callie was a sweet girl most of the time, but since getting pregnant she was growly and grumpy. Luckily for all of them, she only had six more months to go.

As he pulled up to the gate and punched in the numbers to open it, he looked out over the land they all shared. Each of the boys was given a lot of land on the home place, for their own, when they'd turned eighteen. He hadn't done much with his spot yet since he worked so close to the main lodge most days. But he had his own cabin near the back of the main compound. It was cozy, warm, and all his. He didn't have to put up with shit from his family for coming and going at all hours of the night. He especially liked it that way.

His other home away from home was a small office off the back of the barn. He used it for keeping track of the horses—their bloodlines, where they were in their training, the cost to purchase and price sold if they ever got rid of one. Of course, he also had to put up with his brothers using the barn for their little getaway place from time to time. Their old barn had seen its share of raunchy sex.

Moonlight lit the way to the barn as he parked his truck and got out. Leaves rustled overhead in the evening breeze. He really did love the old place. It had such character. The big main lodge housed several rooms they rented out to guests, but it was also where his parents had their rooms. Two of his brothers had once had rooms upstairs, but now that they were married, they'd built their own homes on their piece of land. None of them lived near the main lodge anymore. It made it kind of lonely actually, but quiet and peaceful too.

When he started walking down the path from the parking lot to the barn, he felt eyes on him. It was a strange feeling, but not unusual around there since they did have some resident ghosts on the place.

The barn loomed in the darkness ahead of him. Someone had left the main lights on in the building, illuminating the dirt path that led to the tack room and his apartment. A horse stomped its foot. *Bang. Bang. Bang.* One the horses were apparently disgruntled with being inside on such a pretty night. He smiled. Most people would have attributed that to the ghosts. He knew it was one of the animals kicking at their stall.

He opened the door to his office, flipped on the lights, and then turned off the lights to the barn, plunging the place into darkness before he shut the door to his place.

He had a little work to do on the files before he called it a night. One of the mares was getting ready to foal and he wanted to make sure his paperwork on her was up-to-date, but he also had a new animal he was getting ready to break in the next few days. *My exciting life.* He chuckled as he sat down in his office chair and flipped on the computer.

"Settle down, hell. I'm too young. I don't need a wife and a bunch of kids yet."

He glanced at the ceiling and prayed God wasn't laughing at him. The old adage was tell God about your plans and watch what happens when he laughs. God has his own plans for your future and it usually didn't look anything like what you had in mind.

Chapter Two

The afternoon heat left Joey breathless as he drove down the road toward town. The air conditioning in his truck didn't work at the moment, and he was about to die from the ninety plus heat index. Normal temperatures for this area were ninety or better, so he should be thankful it wasn't hotter today. The run to the feed store had to be done, but he wished now he would have done it in the cooler morning temps. He would survive though. The pool at the ranch sounded really good right about now.

He rounded the corner on the road only to be met with a nasty scene. A motorcyclist had hit a deer, unusual in itself because deer didn't usually move around much in the heat of the afternoon.

He parked his truck on the side of the road and got out. Obviously, the accident had happened in the last few moments because no one else was anywhere close. The motorcycle was torn into several pieces as he stopped near the shattered bike. He glanced left and then right, looking for the rider and/or anybody else who might have been on the bike with the rider. The deer lay twitching on the side of the road. He took out the pistol on his waist and shot the deer in the head. No use making the animal suffer.

"Help. God, please help me."

Joey ran several yards up the road and across the ditch on the side to find a man with his helmet off, bleeding from a gash in his head. His right leg was turned at an odd angle.

"Are you hurt badly?"

"Fuck. I don't know. I can't move my leg."

Joey heard another car coming up the road. "Hang tight. I hear another car. I'll call for emergency and we will see what we can do until they get here. Don't move."

"Hurry."

Joey sprinted back toward the road and noticed a blue four door sedan slowing down. He moved toward the car to see if the person had an emergency kit. He'd taken his out the other day and had forgotten to replace it.

He knocked on the window and was shocked when the driver rolled it down. "Clarissa?"

"Joseph. What's going on?" she asked, opening her door. "What can I do to help?"

"Do you have a blanket or something? A motorcyclist hit a deer. He's pretty messed up over there on the ground. He's bleeding badly from his head and his leg looks like it might be broken."

"I'll grab my stuff from the trunk and see to him. You call 911 and get an ambulance out here."

"Right." Joey grabbed his cell phone from his belt holder and dialed emergency assistance. He told them all he could about the condition of the guy and what had happened, which wasn't much, but as least they were on the way. He headed back to where he'd left the guy only to find Clarissa holding pressure on a wound inside his shirt. "Emergency is on the way. Should be here within a couple of minutes." Blood coated her hands. "Is he going to be okay?"

"I don't know. He's got a bad head wound, a broken leg more than likely, and an abdominal wound that's open and bleeding. It's the worst of his injuries, so I'm holding pressure on it as best as I can."

"I'm glad you came by."

"Me too. I hope he makes it." She glanced down. "He's unconscious now. He's lost a lot of blood."

"They'll fly him out if they need to."

"They probably will have to. He's hurt pretty badly." Clarissa pushed her hair back with her shoulder.

Within a few short minutes, he could hear sirens wailing as they came up the road. "I'll go flag them down and direct them."

"Good idea."

He jumped over the ditch and stopped at the edge of the gravel, waving his hands in the air. A firetruck and ambulance came to a screeching halt, spraying gravel around them as they stopped.

"Where is the patient?"

"Over there in the pasture. You'll have to go through the fencing. It's barbed wire."

"Got it."

"There is a trauma nurse with him. She was on the road and stopped."

"Thank you."

"You're welcome." Joey stood back as he watched the paramedics and fireman go across the ditch, work their way through the fencing, and disappear over the rise where the guy was laying. He hoped the guy was okay. He didn't like seeing anyone hurt like that. Unfortunately, it was a concern out here on the back roads, especially for a motorcyclist.

It wasn't too long before they came dragging the guy out, strapped to the stretcher with something holding his head in place, one paramedic holding pressure on the guys belly, and Clarissa bringing up the rear. Her clothes had dirt streaks on the thighs of her jeans, her hair had come out of the ponytail she had at the back of her head, and her blouse had a tear in it from where she must have snagged it on the fence when she went through.

As they loaded the guy into the ambulance, Clarissa moved to his side, removed the gloves she'd put on her hands, and tossed them into the truck of her car. "Not the way I wanted to spend my day off."

"I bet."

She smoothed back her hair, fixed her ponytail, and then let her arms drop to her sides as she sighed. "I could use something to drink. I guess I'll drive back into town."

"Hey, how about having lunch with me?"

"I don't know, Joseph."

"No pressure. Just lunch between friends." He nodded to the ambulance as it flipped a u-turn in the road, and went screaming back toward town. "You probably saved that guy's life back there. It deserves someone buying you lunch."

"All in a day's work."

"Not on your day off, though." He touched her shoulder. "Come on. Let me buy you lunch at the diner. Besides, I get a family discount there." He grinned as she smiled.

"All right. I have a spare scrub top in my trunk. I'll change at the diner."

"I'll meet you there."

When he pulled up to the diner about fifteen minutes later, he was surprised that there weren't too many people there. In fact, there only seemed to be one or two cars in front.

After he got out of his truck, he shut the door with a bang, and stepped up on the curb. Clarissa pulled her car into the spot next to him.

"You know, I've never eaten here," she said, when she reached his side.

"Really? You are in for a treat then."

"Is this owned by your family?" she asked as he opened the door for her and followed her inside.

"Sort of. It belongs to my aunt on my mother's side."

"Joey!" Anne called from behind the counter. "What brings you in?"

"A friend and I are here to get some food and a cold drink."

Anne nodded as she smiled. "Sit anywhere, honey, and I'll bring you some menus."

He placed his hand at the small of Clarissa's back, guiding her toward a booth to the right. He loved Anne's diner. It was decorated in the fifties style with chrome everywhere, red seats, and white tables. She hadn't changed a thing since she opened it back in the sixties when they'd first moved to Bandera.

He slid into one side of the booth while Clarissa stayed standing at the table. "I need to go wash up, change my shirt and comb my hair."

"Sure. The restrooms are to the back and around that corner."

"I'll be right back."

She disappeared as Anne approached the table and put two menus down. "Do you know what your friend wants to drink?"

"No."

"I'll come back in a second then."

When Clarissa returned, Anne took their drink order while they decided on what to eat.

The bacon cheeseburger sounded good to him. It was his favorite anyway, and he figured after the afternoon they'd had, he deserved a juicy, greasy hamburger with cheese, lettuce, tomato, bacon, and onion with fries on the side. He set his menu down, glancing around the diner while Clarissa made up her mind what she wanted to eat. He could see the two of them becoming good friends.

As his gaze did a thorough sweep of the place, he noticed a red-haired woman sitting alone at one of the tables by the window. She appeared to be writing or drawing something on a large pad of paper. *Odd for this area.* He'd never seen her around here before. She was different enough that he would have noticed her should she be a local. Since he'd lived here all his life, he would know her if she was.

She glanced out the window, then would run the pencil over the paper before looking outside again. He figured she must be drawing something that had caught her attention in their quaint little town.

Clarissa put her menu down. "I think I'll have a French dip. I love those things."

"Anne makes good ones, too, with lots of roast beef."

"Wonderful."

He looked at Clarissa for a moment before his gaze was drawn back to the redhead. Curiosity got the better of him as Anne came back to the table to take their order. When she'd written down what they wanted, he asked, "Who's the woman by the window?"

"I don't know. She came in a few hours ago, ate lunch, and has been sketching ever since. Nice girl, from what I can tell, but she's not from around here."

"I gathered that since I don't know her, and I pretty much know everyone in Bandera."

"You didn't know me, Joseph, when we met at The Dusty Boot last night."

"True. If she just moved here, I probably wouldn't know her then." He looked across the diner again, noticing her gaze fixed outside. "Do you know what she's sketching?"

"No. She hides it every time I get close."

"Hmm. Interesting."

Anne disappeared back behind the counter as he sipped on his Coke.

Clarissa tried bringing up conversation as they sat in the booth waiting for their food, but for some reason, his attention wouldn't stay off the redhead for long.

When she turned and their eyes met, he felt like he'd been kicked in the chest by a horse. Her eyes were a bright green with long eyelashes curled up away from her eyes, framed by black square glasses that made her eyes look bigger. Her cheeks were brushed with pink that darkened the longer he looked. Her red hair hung to her waist in a riot of curls it appeared she tried to tame with a hair tie. Her lips lifted in a tiny smile before she turned away and concentrated on her pad again.

His breath rushed back into his lungs like he'd been underwater way too long.

What the hell?

He'd never reacted to someone like that before, never.

"Are you okay, Joseph? You look really pale."

He shook his head as he focused back on Clarissa. "I'm okay. I just had a really weird reaction to someone, and I'm kind of at a loss as to how to explain it." *I need to keep my focus on my dining partner, not the mystery woman across the room.*

Anne arrived with their plates, giving him more of a reason to concentrate on the woman with him.

Their food looked wonderful, as always. Joey squirted some ketchup onto his burger, squished the bun down so he could fit it into his mouth, and then picked it up to take a bite. Clarissa laughed as he pushed a huge bite of food between his lips.

"Hungry?" Clarissa asked, fixing her own food to her liking before she scooped up a bit of ketchup on her fry and stuffed it into her mouth.

He chewed for a moment and swallowed. "Yes. I haven't eaten today since I slept in this morning."

"You didn't have to work today?"

"Not in a sense. I did have to make a run to the feed store to get something, but I didn't have rides to do." He stuck a french fry into his mouth. "What are your plans for the rest of the day?"

"I don't know. I thought I might wander a bit. I didn't have to work and felt a bit restless. That's why I was out on the back road." She glanced at her watch. "Wow. I didn't realize it was getting so late in the afternoon. My boyfriend will be home from work soon and if I'm not there, he'll flip."

"You don't have to tell him everywhere you go, do you?"

"Nah, nothing like that. He doesn't mind my need to roam as long as he has an idea of where I am. I'd better go though, we have plans." She scooted out of the booth and got to her feet as she grabbed her wallet. "Besides it looks as if you may have another admirer."

As if that was anything new.

"I got it, Clarissa."

"Are you sure?"

"Yeah. I asked you to lunch so my treat."

She smiled as she leaned in a kissed him on the cheek. "You're sweet. I hope you find a nice girl someday soon."

"Thanks."

She gave him another nod of her head before she disappeared out the door of the diner. He hoped they could continue to be friends. He'd like that.

When he focused back on the inside of the diner and not the girl who'd just walked out the door, he was surprised to find the redhead staring at him. Her eyes were wide, her lips were parted slightly, and her right hand was posed over her pad. She broke the contact of their gazes as she looked back down at her paper, her hand moving quickly over the pad.

Curiosity got the better of him as he got to his feet and made his way to her side. "Hi."

She jumped as she pressed the pad to her chest. "Hello."

"I noticed you were drawin' on your pad. Can I ask what you're drawin'?"

Her bottom lip disappeared between her teeth for a moment as she glanced around the diner like she was looking for an escape. "I don't usually show people my drawings."

"If you don't want to, that's okay." He grabbed the chair across the table from her, flipped it around and straddled it. "My name is Joseph Young."

"It's nice to meet you. I'm Rose Gilbert."

"You aren't from here. I can tell by your accent." She smiled and his breath truly caught in his throat. Her whole face lit up when she smiled.

"No, I'm not."

"Are you just visitin'? Do you have family here?"

"No, actually I don't. I'm here on business for the company I work for." She glanced behind him before her gaze came back to him. "Did your girlfriend leave?"

"My who?"

"Your girlfriend. I saw you eating with that dark haired woman."

"Oh, Clarissa? She's not my girlfriend. She's just a friend. I met her at The Dusty Boot last night and we kind of ran into each other today."

"The Dusty Boot?"

"It's the local watering hole or cowboy bar. It's where all the cowboys hang out."

"Ah, I see." She looked out the window for a second before her gaze came back to him. "Sounds nice."

That kicked in the chest feeling came back as he forced his breath out in a whoosh. He chuckled as he pushed his hat back on his head. "Not really. It's pretty rowdy on the weekends, but yeah, we all go there for a good time."

The conversation lagged a little before she blurted out, "Are you a real cowboy?"

"Depends on what you mean by real cowboy? If you mean do I ride horses, mend fences, break new horses to ride, and brand cattle, then yeah, I'm about as real as they come."

"Wow," she whispered, her voice almost reverent in its tone. "I've seen several people walking around town with the same clothing on."

He looked out the window himself for a moment, noticing the people of town walking around. Some went across the street to the bank, others went to the grocery store on the corner, and still more drove down the main street in their trucks. He hadn't realized how it might look to someone not from here. "That's how people dress in Texas."

"It's fascinating."

"Where did you say you're from again?"

"New York. I've never been out of the state before this."

"Well, welcome to Texas, darlin'."

* * * *

Rose's toes curled in her shoes when she heard Joseph say darlin'. Holy crap, he had the cowboy thing down to a science, but if he's a real cowboy, that made sense.

She took in everything about him from the top of his worn cowboy hat to the dusty boots on his feet. He was over six feet tall of solid muscle from what she could see. He had dark hair that peeked out under his hat and curled around his neck, making her want to run her fingers through the thickness. The light blue T-shirt he had on stretched tight over the muscles of his chest and strained against the bulging muscles of his arms. He obviously worked hard every day to have a body like that. His brown eyes reminded her of dark chocolate and when they crinkled at the corners, she could tell he laughed a lot and enjoyed life. *Probably a player then.* Players were something she didn't have time for. She had a purpose in Bandera and it didn't include getting tied up with a local cowboy.

Besides, she probably wasn't his type anyway. With her unruly red hair and thick glasses, she was the persona of nerd. Guys like him didn't go for girls like her. He probably liked his women with tight jeans, big boobs, big blonde hair, and blue eyes. She'd seen lots of pictures of women in Texas and she certainly didn't fit in at all.

Her job sent her to this remote area to get soil and water samples to study the microorganisms that grew in this area. Being a microbiologist was really boring for most people, but it fascinated her like nothing else. She loved to get things under her microscope and figure out what bacteria might be growing in a certain environment. Bandera was mostly cattle ranches, and as such, the Environmental Protection Agency was interested in the effects these animals were having on the water and soil.

"So what brings you to our little town?"

"Work."

"What kind of work do you do?"

She blushed when she thought about how boring her job really was to someone like him. For crying out loud, he broke horses for a living. "I'm a microbiologist."

"Really? That's important work."

"Yes, it is." He smiled and her heart stopped before it jumped into beating again. She rubbed her hand over her stomach where it seemed to be fluttering like crazy. "I, uh…"

"How long have you been doing that kind of work?"

"Two years."

"I've never met a scientist before." He glanced down at her sketch pad where she'd absently laid it down on the table. He craned his head a little as he looked at the sketch. "Is that me?"

"Well, uh, yeah."

"Can I see it?"

"I suppose."

He turned it around so he could see the picture better. "Wow. That's a great likeness. You're very talented."

"Thanks. I only draw for my own pleasure and relaxation. It helps me unwind."

"What other stuff were you drawin'?"

One of her shoulders lifted in a shrug as she felt the heat of a blush rush across her cheeks. Ah, the life of a redhead. "People in town. The town itself with the stoplights and things. Nothing special."

His gaze came back to her. "Can I look at those too? I wouldn't want to be out of line by looking if you don't want me to."

Her heart thumped against her chest, fluttering like a butterfly trapped in a cage. "No, it's fine. They aren't very good since it's only a pencil sketch," she said as he flipped to the next picture and then the next.

"Do you paint?"

"Some."

"I don't know a whole lot about art, but these are really good."

She couldn't help but smile at his compliment. He would never be a New York critic or anything, but somehow his pleasure at her drawings meant more than any critic. "Have you ever been to New York?"

"Nope. My travels are limited to Texas mostly with a few trips to Oklahoma." He closed her sketch pad and focused on her face.

Wow. She could hardly breathe. Her palms felt sweaty and her whole body hummed with awareness of the man sitting so close. She'd never had a reaction to another human being like this before. It felt weird and exciting at the same time. It made her anxious in a way that was very new to her. She always thought she would meet and marry some sophisticated banker, lawyer, doctor, or something along those lines. A guy in a worn cowboy hat, dirty boots, and tight jeans wasn't on her radar at all.

She reached up and adjusted her glasses on her face. It was a nervous gesture, but she needed something to do with her hands. "Does all of Texas look like this?"

He laughed. "Not at all. Some of it's flat. You can see for miles. Hill country like this area is hilly."

"What about the weather? I hear it's really hot here in the summer."

"It is, but the winters can be cold, too."

"I see you made a new friend, Joseph."

He tipped his head toward her, and said, "This is Rose, Aunt Anne."

"Your aunt?"

"Yes, ma'am, on my mother's side."

"Wow. That's cool."

Anne smiled at them and Rose could see the resemblance. "Can I get you two something to drink, more coffee or a Coke?"

He looked up at the older woman standing near their table. "I'll take another Coke, please."

"Yeah, I'll take one too."

"Coming right up."

Anne returned a moment later with two fresh glasses of Coke. "Here ya go."

"Thanks, Aunt Anne."

"You're welcome, nephew." She smiled as she walked away from the table.

"Have you lived here your whole life?" she asked Joseph, fascinated by him and the area they lived in. Her parents had always lived in New York, but that was different. They hadn't lived in the same place within the state more than a few years before moving again either closer to the city or farther out when her dad got a hair up his ass about living in the country.

"Yes, ma'am. Been here since I was born. My parents bought a ranch outside of town when my older brothers were little. The rest of us were born here."

"Rest of you?"

"Yep. I have eight older brothers."

"Holy shit." She covered her mouth as she blushed hard. "I'm sorry," she whispered, afraid she'd offended him in some way. When he chuckled, she realized he'd probably heard a lot worse.

"It's okay. I hear worse than that all the time. Remember nine brothers in a predominantly male household."

"Your mother probably has no hair raising all of you."

He smiled, showing off straight white teeth and a dimple in his cheek. "Actually, she's one tough lady. She had to be with all of us, but especially since three of my brothers are triplets."

"I'd love to meet her. I can't even imagine raising triplets much less six other boys in the mixture."

"I can arrange that."

"Really? I would love to see a real working ranch. Sketching horses would be fantastic."

"If you're free this afternoon, I can take you out there."

"Are you sure? I wouldn't want to impose."

"Darlin', it's a working ranch, yes, but it's also a guest ranch. We have folks around almost all the time, who are staying with us."

She slipped her sketch book into her large bag by her feet. "I'm free for you to do with as you wish."

His eyebrows went up to his hairline as a tiny little grin spread across his lips. "Anything?"

Her face flushed with heat. "Well, almost anything."

"I'm game, honey. I'll give you the executive tour." They both climbed to their feet as he threw some money down on the table.

"What are you doing?"

"Buying your lunch or breakfast, whatever it was."

"You can't do that."

"Why not?"

"Well, I—" She hesitated a moment. "You shouldn't, that's all."

"I want to."

"But then I'll be obligated to you."

He tilted his head to the side and said, "For a little thing like buying you a meal?" He shook his head. "You won't owe me anything other than the joy of your company, Rose."

"Are you sure?"

"Yes, ma'am." He picked up her ticket, handed it and the money to Anne, and then moved to her side. "I would be honored to show you Thunder Ridge."

"I can't wait."

Chapter Three

They drove through big wrought iron gates with a huge TR right in the middle, a little bit later. Joseph had convinced her to leave her car at the diner and take his truck out to the ranch. He insisted it wasn't far from Bandera, so it would be no trouble returning her to town when they were finished.

Rose could feel her heart thumping loudly in her chest as they passed onto the land. Junipers and scrub brush lined the gravel driveway they crept along. Pasture land stretched for a long time in both directions, lined by barbed wire fencing. She couldn't believe her eyes when her gaze stopped on the cattle off to the left. "Oh my. Are those longhorn cattle?"

"Yes. We raise them on the ranch, but these that are out here are like pets. We have more up in the hills that we take to market." He stopped the truck and pointed toward one that was white with brown spots. "See that one right there?"

"Yes," she whispered, in awe of the huge animal.

"He's been on the ranch for the longest. He's almost as old as I am."

"Wow. What's his name?"

"Randy."

She giggled as she pressed her fingertips to her lips. "Really? Randy?"

"Yes, ma'am."

When he turned to look at her, her breath stopped in her throat. The pride on his face made it even more handsome. "He's gorgeous."

"He's randy most of the time, even for his age."

She smiled as she thought about that for a moment, wondering how many little cows he'd made. Cows. Hmm. Was that what they called baby cows? She might have to ask Joseph since she didn't know the first thing about ranching, cows, horses or anything closely resembling the cowboy thing. Talk about being out of her comfort zone. "This is fantastic."

The truck moved slowly forward as she watched the cows continue to graze on the lush green grass beneath their feet. *Feet? I have no idea what they are really called.*

As she turned to look out the front windshield, she was shocked to see a huge two story ranch house come into view. It had a solid rock side with a big wooden door. The porch on the front of the building wrapped all the way around two sides with rockers strategically placed to enjoy. Old farming implements took up residence on the lawn. There were several smaller buildings that complimented the main house, but they were more wood cabin like in design, and were situated a few feet away. A huge barn sat in the distance with fenced off areas situated behind it and to the right. Majestic horses in many different colors stood tied to the posts as if waiting for their owners.

"Wow."

Joseph smiled as he pulled his truck into the parking area, put it in park, and hopped out to open her door.

A gentleman who opens your door for you? I must be in some fairytale or something. Dreaming maybe?

"Thank you."

He tipped his hat.

She sighed.

The gravel crunched under her tennis shoes as they walked to the pathway that led to the main house. She was definitely out of her element here in this atmosphere.

When they approached the wooden door on the side of the building, he pulled it open and motioned for her to go inside.

Pandemonium was the only way she could describe the scene before her. There had to be fifty people laughing, eating, and socializing, the huge room an explosion of noise.

Joseph moved to her side, talking close to her ear. The warmth of his breath on the shell of her ear had her body exploding in goose bumps from head to toe. Even her hair tingled from the sensation.

"We probably should have waited to come out here. There's a large group of writers here this weekend, with my sister-in-law. She's a writer."

"Really? What's her name?" she asked, spinning around to face him before turning back around to search the group. Getting to talk to one of her favorite romance writers would be the epitome of cool.

"Mesa West is what she writes under."

"Oh my God! Seriously? I love her stuff."

"Yes." He placed his hand at the small of her back to guide her forward. "We can go into the main room or into one of the suites upstairs if you want something a bit quieter."

"No. This is exciting." She glanced around the room, taking in all the people who were talking in small groups, leaving very little space to walk. "I can't wait to see the rest of the house."

"Well, this is main dining room where all the meals are served to the guests at the ranch. There are rooms upstairs for people to sleep as well as the cabins you saw outside. The big barn out back is for the horses. It's where I spend most of my time."

"Can we see the other room?"

"Sure." He motioned for her to precede him through the arched doorway into the main room.

There was a huge rock fireplace to the left with big bookcases rising almost to the ceiling. Three big leather couches were positioned near the fireplace with several individual lounge chairs scattered around the room. An old piano stood against one wall.

She took in the entire room, absorbing the atmosphere and the ambiance of the lifestyle. The whole thing held her spellbound.

"My mother's office is right there in the corner and the one farther down the hall is my brother Jonathan's. He's the marketing person and website guru."

"What do your other brothers do around here besides ride horses?"

He motioned for her to follow him to another small room where there were a couple of leather loveseats, things for sale, and thankfully, doors that could be closed. As she found a comfortable spot to sit, he pulled the glass sliding door shut, leaving them in blessed silence.

"This is very nice."

"Can I get you something cold? There are Cokes in here as well as some wine if you'd like."

"It's a little early for wine, but a Coke would be great. Thank you."

Joseph reached into the cooler in the corner and pulled out a can of Coke to hand to her. "Here you go."

He took a seat next to her.

After she'd quenched her thirst, she set the can on the small table to her right before she turned to face him again. "So, what's your typical day like?"

"I'm up by six normally. I feed and water the horses, brush them all down, clean their hooves, and saddle them for the day."

"Do they stand around all day in that heavy leather?"

"Yes, but we don't cinch them until we know someone is about to go out for a ride. The saddles are on their backs, but not tight."

"Oh. That's good. I wouldn't want to be standing around in the heat of the summer with those heavy blankets and bulky load on."

"We take very good care of our animals."

"What else do you do?"

"Sometimes I take riders out. We usually go for an hour unless it's a special ride that has been booked in advance to go out longer. I also help maintain the tack for the animals, the saddles, bridles, and such."

"If you hadn't guessed, I know absolutely nothing about horses, what you called tack, or how to take care of a horse."

"Horses are great animals. They are very affectionate with people they know. They love to please. We have several different breeds here including quarter horses, Arabians, Morgans, Mustangs, Paints, Saddlebreds, and so on."

She couldn't help but laugh since she had no idea what any of those types of horses were. Born and raised in New York had its perks and drawbacks, not having a clue about the country lifestyle was one of them.

"What do your brothers do on the place?"

"Jeff is the eldest. He's the foreman around here. Jackson is second in line. He's married to a country singer, so he's not around a lot anymore, but he does some wrangling when he's home. Jacob is third. He helps around the place too. Like most of my brothers, he has his own place now and does his own thing. Jason, Joel, and Joshua are the triplets. Joel is married to Mesa who is the writer. Jason is married to Peyton who is a bartender at The Dusty Boot and Joshua is married to Candace. She does a lot with websites. All three of them have their own houses, but help out around the home place during roundup, branding, and whatever else. Jonathan recently got engaged to one of the women who works here. Her name is Mandy and she's good friends with Peyton, and then there is Jeremiah. He's married to Callie. They were friends in high school, but got together not too long ago. Jeremiah is the financial planner for the ranch. He watches all the money that goes in and out of here."

"Holy crap. Sounds like a very busy place to be."

"Yeah, sometimes it's hard to get alone time around here." He chuckled as he put his arm across the back of the sofa, crossed one leg over the other so his ankle was on the opposite knee, and relaxed against the arm behind him. "So tell me what you do when you aren't hunting bacteria."

She blushed thinking how boring her life sounded in comparison to what went on here. "I study bacteria under a microscope, differentiating the various types, what they do, and how they affect their environment, like water and soil."

"I'm impressed."

"You are?"

"Yeah. I've never really talked to a scientist before. I mean, I took biology in high school, of course, but I've never been to college like some of my brothers. I'm just a cowboy."

She laid her palm on his foot. "That's a very important job, Joseph. You do what you do to make it safe for people to come here, have a good time, and not worry about being hurt."

He shrugged one shoulder. "Most of the time, I feel like I don't matter all that much. Being the baby of the family makes me feel like I'm replaceable, you know?"

"I'm sure you aren't at all. You are a very important part of this operation if you are the only one who is responsible for the animals here. Didn't you say you break the new horses you buy, as well?"

"Yes."

"That's a dangerous thing to do all the time. Have you been hurt before?"

"Yeah. I broke my leg when I was like twelve." He shuddered before focusing back on her face. "It wasn't a pleasant experience. I hate hospitals."

She smiled and dropped her gaze to the coffee table top. It was very unique. Kind of a mosaic top with a wood base that had little spots burnt into it. She'd never seen anything similar in her life. Then again, this whole cowboy thing was new to her.

When she raised her gaze again, there were frown lines between his dark eyebrows. "Yet you continue to do it."

"Well, yeah. It's my job and I haven't been hurt in a long time. I'm very careful when I ride or break in a new horse."

"How does one break in a new horse?"

"It's a slow, meticulous process. We put them in a smaller pen, work with them to gentle them, and break them to halter first."

She shook her head and grinned. "It's like you are talking a foreign language to me. What's a halter?"

He tried showing her with his hands. "It's usually made of nylon. You put it on their nose and then back behind their ears." He laid his hands back down and shrugged. "It would be much easier to just show you."

She jumped to her feet. "Okay!"

"Like right now?"

"Of course. Show me what you do."

He climbed to his feet with a grin on his lips. "All right then. Follow me."

Excitement quickened her steps as she followed him back through the throng of people in the main lodge and dining room, out the side door, and across the lawn to the big red structure toward the back. The smells surrounding her were intriguing. The scent had a sweet aroma to it, from what she wasn't sure. Sweat, dirt, and grass smells assaulted her senses as they approached the big double doors.

When they moved through and down the long dirt hall, she noticed several smaller areas that had short, sliding half doors on them with bars on the tops. "What are those?"

"Stalls. We keep the horses in them at night."

She stopped to look inside, disappointed there were no animals to peek at.

"The horses are all out in the paddock right now."

"Paddock?"

He smiled, showing off a small dimple in his cheek. "I forget that you have no idea what I'm talking about. The lingo to me is natural, but for someone who has never been around horses or farm animals, you are totally lost."

She nodded as she moved back to his side. "You'll have to explain it to me."

"Paddocks are small areas that are designated to hold the horse while they are waiting for riders. Ours is a long, wide area where we tie them."

"They have food and water, right?"

He frowned. "Of course. We don't neglect our animals."

"I didn't say you did. It just occurred to me that they are unable to get water and stuff for themselves if they are tied to a pole or whatever."

"I'm sorry. It bothers me when folks think we don't take care of our horses. They are well fed, brushed daily, bathed regularly, and exercised even if they aren't out on a ride. My brothers and I switch out which animals we ride when we are taking a group out. That way all of them are ridden regularly. We don't want any of them to get ornery with a guest since most of the guests aren't experienced riders."

As they continued down the walkway, she noticed a large covered area off to the side. "What's that for?"

"It's where we work the horses sometimes or when I have to break one, I'll take it in there to work with it so that I can keep it contained. Wild horses can be difficult to break. They aren't used to being around people."

"Do you have a lot of wild horses on your property?"

"No. We buy them from auction most of the time. The only thing roaming our land is our guests, our horses, and our cattle."

"Is that what you call the long-horn one out there in the front?"

"Yes. Cows are referred to as cattle."

"What are baby cows called?"

"Calves."

"Baby horses?"

"Foals until they are a year old. A girl horse is a mare. A boy horse that has been fixed so he can't make babies is a gelding. A boy horse that still is able to make babies is a stud. A baby female horse is a filly and a baby male horse is a colt."

"Wow." She glanced up into the rafters of the barn. "What's up there?"

"Our hayloft. We keep the extra hay we have for the horses, up there."

"I bet it's fun up there."

He shrugged as a small grin appeared on his lips. "It can be."

"Have you ever had sex in the hayloft?"

He choked and coughed as he blushed a deep red. "Well now, I don't go around discussing my sex life with strangers, but it has been used a time or two by those in the family."

She liked that he was a bit embarrassed by discussing his sex life. Most guys were very open and boastful about how many women they'd been with. It was cute.

The scent of leather met her nose. "Where is the leather scent coming from?"

"Our tack room near the back. We keep all our saddles, bridles, bits, and other riding equipment back there."

"Can I see it? I love the smell of leather."

"Sure," he said, leading her to the end of the dirt walkway, past all the stalls to the door that was shut. He knocked loudly for a moment, before entering.

"Why did you knock?"

"My brother, Jeremiah, has his office in there." He looked down at the floor as he scuffed the dirt with the toe of his boot. "He and Callie sometimes go in there to be alone so I always knock."

No sound came from the room.

He slowly turned the door handle and peered inside. "It's safe."

She giggled as she pressed her fingertips to her lips. The thought of bursting in on a couple was almost funny. She could totally imagine how hard it would be to get some alone time in a place like this, with so many people around all the time.

When they stepped into the large room, she noticed wooden things on the wall. Some had saddles on them and some were empty. "What are those?" She pointed to the leather contraption with a metal thing hanging crossways in the middle of it.

"Bridles." He took one off the hook and showed it to her. "This part goes in the horse's mouth, this part goes behind their ears, and these go around their neck so the rider can guide them where they want them to go."

"Sounds complicated."

"Not really." He put it back on the hook before he took down another piece. "This is a halter." He stretched one part open. "This goes over their nose and this part goes behind their ears."

"What is it for?"

"It's to help catch them when they are in an open area. It's not uncomfortable for them or anything, but with a lead rope hooked to the ring under their chin, it makes it easier to lead them where we need them to go."

"I see." She glanced down at the bucket on the floor with several things in it. "What are those for?"

"They are different brushes we use to groom them." He picked up a metal hook. "This is to clean their hooves with."

"Why do you have to do that?"

"We make sure they are in good condition, no sores or that they don't have any rocks that could hurt their hoof after they've gone out on rides. Sores on their feet are really bad for horses. We're constantly checking them to make sure they aren't developing anything within the hoof."

"Caring for them is a lot of work."

"Yes it is." He swept out his hand toward the door. "Let me show you the animals we have out in the paddock."

"I would love to see them." She grinned as she went through the door and then waited for him to shut it behind them before walking in front of her through a doorway a little ways down and off to the right.

When they stepped out into the sunshine, she was partially blinded by the glare. He grabbed a straw cowboy hat from the rack to their left, plopping it on her head. The wide brim of the hat shaded her eyes enough that she could see around her.

He grinned as he tapped the brim of the hat. "You look cute."

"Thanks." She winced. "I guess."

"Now all you need are jeans and boots and you'll look like a regular cowgirl."

"I'll see what I can do."

He showed her the horses, naming each one, telling her how old they were, what type of horse they were, where the family acquired it, and what kind of temperament it had. "Well, that's all of them except those that are pastured right now. We swap out the herd every so often so that they all get exercise, but also get a chance to rest."

"This is fascinating, Joseph."

"I'm glad you like it."

This all felt very strange to her. She'd just met this man, but it seemed like she'd known him for a long time. Her comfort level around him amazed her. She frowned. She shouldn't be feeling this. She was in love with someone else, wasn't she?

Brandt wouldn't like her being friendly with another man.

"What's wrong?"

"Uh, nothing. Thank you for the tour."

"You're welcome." He rocked back on the heels of his boots as he stuffed his hands in his front pockets. "Would you like to stay for supper?"

This is all research, right? I mean, I need the soil and water samples from the area in different places to get a good variable exposure. "Uh, sure. That sounds like fun."

"I'll warn you, my family can be overwhelming."

"That's okay. I like big families."

"You'll definitely get that with mine."

His warm hand at the small of her back felt safe and comfortable as he guided her back through the barn toward the house.

"It'll be a while before we eat, but you'll hear the dinner bell they ring to let everyone know when the meal is served. Would you like to see more of the property while we wait?"

"I would love to."

He took her hand in his and led her to his truck, opened the door, and then helped her inside with his hands on her waist.

Holy shit! Did this guy just step out of a western romance novel or something?

She wiped the drool from her chin as she watched him walk around the front bumper to the driver's side. Men like this didn't exist, did they?

Apparently in Bandera, Texas they did.

Chapter Four

Joey glanced at the pretty redhead across the cab of his truck before looking back out the windshield. She wasn't the typical cowgirl he normally went out with. It was kind of funny how totally out of her element she seemed. She knew nothing about cattle, horses, or ranching. He guessed he'd feel the same way if he went to her neck of the woods. "What would you like to see?"

"Everything."

He laughed. "That's a tall order." After he backed out of the parking spot, he headed around the back of the cabins to the cattle guard across the north pasture area. They would go around the hills, across the streams, and out by the mud pit where they all wet muddin' on occasion during the summer. The rumble of the cattle guard when his tires went over made her giggle and look at him.

His heart skipped a beat at the pure joy she found in something so simple. Her eyes were wide as her hand gripped the door handle to her right while they took the road to the left. Gravel crunched under the tires as they drove along slowly so she could take it all in. Showing her the sights of his home made him feel powerful and important. It was a brand new feeling to him. He liked it, liked it a lot.

They spent the next two hours roaming around the property belonging to Thunder Ridge. He found some of the cattle grazing in one of the back pastures and stopped so she could watch them.

Seeing things through her innocent eyes had him appreciating what he'd taken for granted for so long. The beauty of the hill country in spring, the large long-horned cattle peacefully munching on the tall grass, the blooming Bluebonnets that made the area explode in bright color, and the peacefulness of the pond where he and his brothers swam as children. Even now, he'd be out riding fences and come up on the pond only to hear the soft sighs and low moans of one of his brothers and their girls spending some alone time.

Realizing he wanted that for himself made him stop with a start.

"Is something wrong?"

"N-no. I'm realizing how the whole area looks through your eyes, someone who has never been here before, and it makes me appreciate it all the more." He stopped several yards away from the pond. "Would you like to see a special spot we swam in as kids?"

She nodded enthusiastically as she turned to open the door, but he stopped her with a hand on her arm.

"Let me get it."

The smile on her lips made his breath catch in his throat. He couldn't wait to see her in the sunshine with the sparkling water of the pond behind her. He knew she would love it as much as he did, maybe more.

After he opened her door, he held out his hand to help her out of the cab of the truck. He knew it was kind of high off the ground. Her head came to about the middle of his nose when she stepped out and stood on the ground. That made her about five-foot-eight, he figured.

Her red hair blew wildly in the spring breeze as she rubbed her arms. He should have thought to have her bring a coat. It got cool up here in the spring sometimes. "Wait right here."

He hurried around to the other side, opened the door, and grabbed his jean jacket that he kept behind his seat.

When he held it out for her to place her arms in, she smiled up at him. Her perfect pink lips parted slightly as he lost himself in her green eyes.

She giggled softly, pushed her arms into the jacket, and spun around so she could wrap it around her.

He kicked himself for being such a sap. Yes, she was beautiful, smart, funny, and good company, but he really didn't need a complication in his life right now. He already had too many women to keep track of besides keeping his ass out of trouble. Jessica's father kept trying to shoot him, Clarissa had a boyfriend and didn't need anyone in her life to complicate things, and Rose wasn't here but for a short time to do a job. Being attracted to her was one thing, but he couldn't act on it. "This way," he said, taking two steps in front of her to lead the way. Why he was showing her this special spot, he wasn't sure since he figured it was a bad idea to get involved with her.

A gasp escaped her mouth as they crested the hill that led down to where the pond was. "This is beautiful, Joseph." She walked on past him, down to the pond's edge.

Sparkling in the sunlight, the water appeared bluer than normal as a few fish swam about. She sat on a rock near the edge and took off her tennis shoe and sock, before sticking her toes in. "It's warm!"

"Yes, it's a warm spring. It stays a constant seventy degrees no matter how hot or how cold it is outside."

"This is magnificent! I wish I had brought a swimming suit. I would go in."

He smiled at her enthusiasm. It was contagious. He moved to sit beside her so he could watch her. Her face lit up with excitement at the area around them. The small sandy beach his dad had made for them, the rocks that surrounded the area, keeping it secluded, the blue water, the small fish, and the sunshine sparkling off the still edges all made for a very pretty spot.

"You used to swim here as a child?"

"Yeah, my brothers and I used to come out here all the time, even in the winter."

"I can't imagine getting out of that warm water into the cold air." She shivered and wrapped the coat tighter around her.

Unable to stop himself, he moved to sit behind her and drew her back between his legs so she could rest against his chest and be warm. "There. Better?"

"Yes, much. Thank you."

He tucked her head under his chin and wrapped his arms around her shoulders, pulling her in tight.

"Joseph?"

"Yeah?"

"How old are you?"

"Thirty-one. Why?"

"Curiosity mostly."

"How old are you?"

"Twenty-six."

"And you are a microbiologist?"

"Yes."

"What kind of schooling does that require? I assume you went to college for it."

"Yep. Four years and a bachelor's degree, but I am planning to finish my Ph.D."

"What's that?"

"My doctorate degree."

"Oh." *Wow*. He felt really stupid. He'd never gone to college. He'd never been anywhere except Texas and Oklahoma. He'd never had a steady girl. He'd never done a lot of things, but here was this girl who was younger than he was, who had a degree, lived in New York, knew about stuff he had no idea about like under a microscope and shit, and he was nothing more than a lowly cowboy. She was totally out of his league and he might as well get that through his thick skull before he did something stupid, like kiss her.

He liked the way she felt in his arms though, tucked into his embrace like she was meant to be there.

Where in the hell did that come from?

"Rose?"

"Yeah?"

"How long are you here for?"

"A few weeks is all. Once I collect the samples I need, I'll be heading back to New York."

"How would you like to stay here at the ranch, collect your samples, and be exposed to some real southern hospitality?"

"What are you asking?"

"I'm asking if you would like to stay on the ranch and hang out with me. I can show you Bandera, San Antonio, Houston or wherever you want to go, give you the royal treatment for the time you're here."

She turned in his arms so she faced him even though she was still sideways in his embrace. Her breath warmed his lips as she stared up into his eyes. Her pupils dilated. Her lips parted. Her breathing sped up as they looked at each other without saying a word.

He wanted to kiss her more than anything.

His fingers tangled in her hair, scraping his fingertips over her scalp, as he slowly drew her closer. When he closed his eyes and drifted toward her mouth, he anticipated the taste of her lips, the softness of the surface, and the pleasure he would feel at the first touch of her mouth. He wasn't prepared for the reaction of his body to the brush of her lips against his. Desire rushed through his blood, exploding in a high he'd never felt before. His head spun. Blood rushed in his ears. His heart sped up until it was pounding in his chest like a runaway freight train.

When she placed her hand on his chest, he thought his heart had stopped. He tilted his head to the side to deepen the kiss as his tongue brushed against her lips seeking her permission to enter her mouth.

She parted her lips slightly, letting him in so his tongue slipped along hers. A soft moan escaped her mouth as he lost himself in her kiss.

His cell phone jingled in his pocket, making him jump, which in turn broke the kiss.

She pulled the jacket tighter around herself and stood as he fished the phone out of his pocket and answered it.

"Hello?"

"Joey, it's Jessica."

"Hey."

"Can I see you tonight? My dad is out of town buying cattle."

He looked at Rose who'd wandered a few feet away, his thoughts in turmoil. "I, uh, I can't, Jess. I have company." Rose wasn't a guarantee of getting sex, but then again neither was Jessica. Yeah, Jessica came on like an experienced woman, but Joey didn't know if she was or not. What happened if she backed out at the last minute? What if her dad had someone watching the place for just this type of situation? No, he needed to stick with Rose even if she wasn't a shoo-in for a great night of sex, besides, he liked her. She wasn't the typical Texas woman. She wasn't from here at all, and it was kind of nice to have that difference.

"Seriously? This is the perfect opportunity for us to have some alone time, and you can't because you have company? What the hell, Joey?"

"Sorry, Jess, but yeah. I'm busy tonight and probably for the next couple of weeks. An old family friend will be spending some time at the ranch, and I've been volunteered to show her around."

"Her?"

"Uh, yeah. She's an old family friend. Matronly even. She's like fifty or something."

"Is everything okay, Joseph? Do we need to go back to the house?" Rose said, her voice clearly carrying over the phone.

"She doesn't sound very matronly to me and exactly where are you that you need to go back to the house?"

"Listen, I gotta go, Jess. I'll talk to you later." He quickly hit the end button on his phone before stuffing it back into his front pocket. Talk about cock blocked. "Everything is fine. We don't have to go back unless you want to, Rose."

"Who is Jess? I didn't think you had any sisters."

"I don't. She's, uh, a friend."

"Oh." Rose headed back to where his truck was parked. "I suppose we should get back anyway."

"Didn't you want to get some samples or something? I mean, we don't have to go back yet." After he looked at the watch on his arm, he shoved his hands in his pockets as he followed behind her. "I was enjoying being out here with you."

She smiled as she leaned against the front bumper. "I gathered that, but no, I can't get my samples right now. I don't have my equipment with me."

"We could go hike up over the hill there, so I can show you more of the area."

"I really don't have hiking shoes on." She glanced down as she wiggled her shoe so he could see the flats she wore. "Cowboy boots, hiking boots. Wow. I need to hit a store before I go anywhere else with you."

He grinned as he stopped in front of her. "I guess you do."

"Isn't it about time for supper at the house?"

"Not really, and come to think of it, I would love to take you out some place for supper, if you'd go with me."

"Oh?"

"Yeah. I could show you San Antonio down on the River Walk. They have some great restaurants down there like Tex-Mex, steak, seafood, or whatever. You pick."

* * * *

"I was kind of looking forward to having supper with your family. I think it would be great to get to know them." A frown pulled down the corners of his mouth making her want to smooth it away with her fingers. *He's too cute to frown.* "We could always do San Antonio tomorrow evening." She reached up to caress the side of his face and smooth out the little lines near his mouth. "Don't frown. It gives you wrinkles."

He shook his head as the corners of his mouth now lifted in a smile. "All right. Tomorrow it is, and after supper, we'll hit The Dusty Boot."

"You really are trying to kill my feet, aren't you?"

"Nope, but you will need to get some boots. You sure can't be seen in the best country bar in Bandera in those. There are names for folks like that."

"There are?"

"Yep."

"What's that?"

"Yankees or honkees."

She started to giggle and as it turned into a full-blown, gut rolling laugh, he joined in. His laughter was contagious as his eyes twinkled with mirth. They continued to laugh until they were both holding their stomachs. "You are too much."

"It's the truth."

After she pushed off the bumper of the truck, she walked around to the passenger side. He followed, opening the door for her to climb back up in the cab. His hands on her waist as he helped her up, felt strange but right in some way. "Thank you."

"You're welcome." He tipped his hat before he shut the door.

Her mind spun as she watched him walk around the front of the vehicle to the driver's side. *There is something weird going on here, and I'm not sure what. I have a boyfriend, one I thought I was in love with, but this attraction to Joseph is making me have second thoughts about my relationship with Brandt. How can I be attracted to someone this strongly? I really need to break things off with Brandt if I'm having these second thoughts.*

"You okay?"

"Yes, why?"

"You look lost in thought." He turned the key, bringing the truck to life with a roar of the diesel engine before he faced her. "I'm sorry if I got a little carried away back there with the kiss and all."

"I didn't mind, and I'm not sorry you kissed me."

"Good."

"Good?"

"Yeah, because I really want to do it again. I didn't want to be out of line though, if you weren't okay with it."

She smiled as she lowered her gaze to where her hands were folded in her lap. She liked Joseph, a lot, but she wasn't the type to cheat. Calling Brandt tonight would be a good idea, so she could clear her heart. After supper when she was back in her hotel room, she'd do it, she'd call him and breakup.

They drove back to the lodge in virtual silence other than a comment now and again about the current song on the radio. She hadn't really appreciated the tunes on country radio until she stopped to listen. The lyrics really spoke to her now that she slowed down to really hear them. Her toe tapped to the beat as her fingers did a little strum on her thigh.

"Enjoying the music?"

"Yes. I listen to some country music, but not a ton. We don't have very many good country stations where I live. I do have a couple that are my favorites though."

"What kind of music do you normally listen to?"

She glanced at him across the cab and said, "Opera and classical mostly. I go to the shows on Broadway sometimes."

His lips stretched into a big grin, showing off that sexy little dimple in his cheek.

"You're laughing at me."

"No, I'm not. I'm realizing how different we are, is all."

They pulled up in front of the main lodge. She noticed a large group of women making their way in through the doors for supper or dinner. She couldn't remember what they called it in the South, but she knew there was a difference. There was no way she would ask Joseph. He would laugh at her again. Then again, she didn't mind seeing his smile. He had a really sexy one.

It wouldn't be dark for a while yet, so she hoped they could still explore near the main lodge a bit or she might be able to help him with the horses for the night.

After he parked the truck and walked around to open her door, they walked up toward the house. He took her hand in his, making her shiver with sensation. Why his touch did this to her, she wasn't sure, but she knew she liked it. Brandt's touch had never caused such a reaction in her, leaving her baffled.

"Cold?"

"Uh, no, not really."

He smiled as he pulled her closer to his side and wrapped his arm around her shoulders. "Just in case."

Snuggling with a hot guy, best place to be in the world.

They walked through the door into the mayhem of supper inside Thunder Ridge. It was a good thing she didn't have any social anxiety because there were a ton of people including his family, all of the guests, and the staff.

"Let's head up by the stairs. That's where the family sits."

Several of the people sitting at the table swiveled their heads around as Joseph escorted her to a chair and held it out for her. She smiled slightly, hoping to ease their obvious curiosity at her appearance at their table. Joseph took the chair next to her.

"Joey?"

"Uh. Everyone, this is Rose Gilbert. She's a friend I've invited to supper." He went around the table introducing his entire family. "And that's my mother, Nina, and my father, James."

"It's very nice to meet you all. I'm sorry, but I won't be able to remember all your names."

"It's fine, honey," Nina replied. "I hope you aren't too overwhelmed with this bunch." Nina turned to the family. "You all behave yourselves tonight and don't frighten this poor girl." She smiled at Rose. "Welcome to Thunder Ridge."

"Thank you."

"Where are you from? You have an accent I'm not familiar with."

"I'm from New York."

"Interesting place. I've been there a time or two."

"Oh? Which part?"

"New York City. I've done a little traveling over the years."

"I like it, but I'm realizing how different Texas is from New York."

"That's the God's honest truth, honey. I do hope you will enjoy our hospitality while you're in the area."

"I'm sure I will. Joseph has shown me parts of your property today. The pond is beautiful."

A few snickers could be heard from the other males at the table. She frowned, wondering why the mention of the pond was so funny.

Nina shot them all a motherly glare, quieting them quickly.

Rose looked down the table, taking in the group as a whole. It was apparent they were all brothers, carrying the same coloring and mostly the same facial features, although she noticed the different eye colors the group had. The triplets were another shocker. They were indeed identical and it kind of threw her off a bit. It was weird to see the same face on three different people. She had to wonder if their wives could tell them apart because she was having a hard time of it. The women all sat by their men with their children close by at another table if they were old enough or in high chairs if they needed to be closer to their parents. They appeared to be a very loving group of people the way they all cuddled their spouses, kissed them, hugged them or had an arm around their shoulders. They were all tall even though some were taller than the others.

Joseph's parents were an interesting pair as well. Nina had the dark coloring of the boys with long black hair and dark eyes while James was lighter in coloring. Nina appeared to have Native American blood somewhere in her lineage, evident by her features. Striking was the only word she could think of for Joseph's mother.

"Joseph?" Jeff said, snickering behind his hand. "Did you break that new mare today?"

She turned to see Joseph glare at his brother down the table wondering at the flare of anger in his gaze. "Actually, no. I had to make a run into town to get feed, remember, and then I met Rose at the diner. I never made it to the breaking paddock. I'll do it tomorrow."

"Did you get the feed?"

"No. I came across a motorcycle verses deer this morning before I could make it there. The guy was pretty messed up. I met a friend on the road who stopped as well, and we went to the diner for lunch. That's where I met Rose. We came out here afterwards. I totally forgot about the feed."

"You'll need to go back into town for it then. We need it tonight."

"Fine."

Jeff grinned as he pulled his wife's hand up to place a kiss to the back of it. Rose melted at the scene. These guys sure seemed to have the gentleman thing down pat. They all had a hand or something on their spouse, making her feel like she might be intruding on a special moment for them.

She cleared her throat as she turned to see most of the guests had retrieved their plates and taken their seats. The family as a whole got up from their chairs and she slowly stood as well, unsure of what was going on.

Joseph leaned in and whispered in her ear, "We can eat now. We always wait for the guests to be served and seated before we eat."

"Ah. I see." She followed Joseph to the line near the serving counter, grabbed a plate from the stack, and allowed the servers to fill it. As she neared the salad, she realized the food was already overflowing and she would never be able to eat it all.

Joseph smiled as he urged her on. "You don't have to eat everything."

"Thank God. My stomach hurts just looking at it all."

They returned to their seats at the table as the conversations flowed around her. Talk centered on cattle, horses, ranch work, the pregnancies of the group and their current cravings, how Samantha's tour was going, and how Mesa's newest book was selling. She hadn't realized there were other famous people within the group until someone mentioned Samantha. "You're Samantha Harris-Young?"

Samantha smiled and nodded.

Rose thought her world had just come full circle. One of her favorite country music singers and one of her favorite romance novelists were part of the same family. "Oh my God! I love your songs. I have your new CD. Heck, I have all your CDs."

"Thank you. I appreciate you being a fan."

"Dang it! I don't have them all with me, or I would have you sign them." She frowned as she looked down the table. "If that wouldn't be too weird, you know."

"No, honey. It's fine." Samantha smiled at Jackson and then back at her. "If you send them to the ranch, I will sign them and send them back to you once you get home."

"I would love that!" Rose glanced at Joseph as he sat next to her grinning from ear to ear. "What?"

"You are too cute."

"I'm not embarrassing you, am I? I'm sorry."

"No, darlin'. It's fine. Samantha is used to it, I'm sure, and after supper, I will introduce you to Mesa. She is sitting with her friends tonight. You might even know some of them that are here."

She grasped his hand and squeezed it. "Thank you."

"I haven't done anything."

"You brought me here. You have no idea how much this means to me."

"I'm glad I could do this for you."

She smiled again before she grabbed her fork and dug into her food. The mixture of spices exploded on her tongue as she tasted the combination of the dish they were eating. She wasn't sure what it was, but it sure was interesting to eat. Then again, she wasn't familiar with the different foods they might be eating in Texas.

"Do you like it?" Nina asked before her fork slid between her lips.

"Yes. It's an interesting combination of flavor. May I ask what it is?"

"We call it Texas Chili. It has a lot of different flavors inside including onion, garlic, beer, jalapenos, cilantro, unsweet chocolate, and several other things." Nina nodded to the tortillas on the plate next to her. "Try ripping off a piece of the tortilla to scoop some up and eat it that way."

Rose nodded, tore off a piece of the flour tortilla and dipped the small piece into the bowl before putting it between her lips. Her mouth tingled from the flavors bursting on her tongue as she chewed and then swallowed the savory food. "Oh my, that is fantastic. Thank you for the tip, Nina." She blushed as she bit her lip for a moment. "Or should I call you Mrs. Young?"

"Oh my goodness, no. Nina is fine, honey. I've never been Mrs. Young to anyone except the folks at the bank when we first got married."

The group laughed, including her, making her feel like part of the family. Thinking that way would get her into trouble though, so she'd better remember her place. A guest is all she was and all she would ever be on this ranch.

Chapter Five

Joey walked her out to the truck so he could take her back to her rental car still parked at the diner. He wished the evening wouldn't end, but it was getting late plus he had plans to see her again tomorrow evening for dinner and some dancing at The Dusty Boot. The thought of holding her in his arms as they swayed on the dance floor had him smiling.

"What are you grinning about?"

"I was thinking about tomorrow evening and how I can't wait to hold you while we dance."

A frown pulled down the corners of her mouth and made a cute little wrinkle appear between her eyebrows.

"What's wrong?"

"I, uh. I don't know how to dance."

"I'm sure you've slow danced before, right?"

"Well, yes, but not a lot. High school was probably the last time I did."

He laughed. "It hasn't changed."

She smacked him on the arm. "I didn't think it had, silly. I don't know how to do all those other dances that you do here."

"You mean two-step?"

"That's one of them, yes."

"I'll teach you."

"Are you sure? I mean, what if I step on your toes?"

"You wouldn't be the first, darlin'."

Silence enveloped them for a moment as he continued down the darkened road toward town. Stars winked in the nighttime sky. The moon shone bright outside the front windshield. Thinking about how soft her lips had been under his when he'd kissed her earlier, had him getting uncomfortably hard in his jeans. Her taste had been intoxicating. The way her mouth molded to his made him think of doing other things with her, things he probably shouldn't be thinking about on such a basic level. Her hair had been so soft in his hand, curling around it like it was meant to be there. *Damn it. I need to get laid, but having Rose right now isn't the answer.*

"It really is beautiful out here. The stars are so bright. You can see millions of them."

"Yep."

"In New York, the city lights are so blinding, you can hardly see the stars at night unless you go outside of the city."

"Do you do that? Go outside the city, I mean."

"Yeah. My parents own a place upstate in a small community where we have a house. It's beautiful there in the summer, cool with a lovely lake nearby, and lots of green trees."

"Sounds nice."

"Maybe I'll be able to show it to you someday."

"I'd like that."

"Me too, Joseph."

He pulled up next to her car in the parking lot of the diner and shut off the engine. They sat in the dark truck for what seemed like a long time. The radio played softly in the background. He turned toward her and took her hand in his. "Thank you for spending the day with me."

A smile spread across her lips. "Thank you for taking me. I haven't had that much fun in a long time. I learned a lot about you and your family. They are great people."

"I appreciate you saying that. Even if they do drive me crazy sometimes, I still love them. I wouldn't trade them for anything."

"I imagine."

"You haven't told me about your family. I know you live in New York, but not much else." He let his hand relax, cradling her palm in his as he laced their fingers together. It felt intimate and he wasn't sure why he was doing it. He wasn't much of a hand holder type. He didn't do the small things for the women he dated, but he sure felt like doing it with her—slow, sensuous kisses, holding hands, stroking her arm, touching her face, rubbing a section of her hair between his fingers.

"We probably don't have time to go into my whole life story tonight." She glanced at the dashboard. The clock read ten.

"It's still early."

"Not really. I've been up since five this morning."

"An early riser. Me too." He shrugged. "Of course, my excuse is usually because of work."

"Mine too, but not this morning. I found myself wanting to see the sunrise over the hills when I woke up in the motel."

"Are staying here in town?"

"Yes. There is a small one not far from downtown and right across from the bar you mentioned."

"The Dusty Boot. Yeah, there is. It's not a bad place, although I've never stayed there."

"No, I imagine you haven't."

She licked her lips, tempting him to kiss her again. He wanted to, very badly. Instead, he looked back out the windshield and the deserted street.

"I should get going."

"Yeah, me too. Sunrise comes early."

"Yes it does."

"What time do you want me to pick you up for supper tomorrow?"

"Uh, four? It's about forty-five minutes to an hour back into San Antonio, right?"

"Yes. I'll make reservations for five then."

"Where are we going?"

"It's a surprise."

She smiled again, reminding him of a flower opening to the morning sunshine. "I love surprises."

"Good." He brought her hand to his mouth, brushing the back of it with his lips. She shivered under his touch. The reaction made his heart pound. She was attracted to him too. The thought had his heart thumping in his ears, but he had to slow this down. His short terms plans had room for fun with a green-eyed redhead. What of his long term plans? Those didn't include a woman, did they? He didn't think so.

He let her go as he opened his door so he could help her out on her side.

When she stepped out, he laid his palm at the small of her back to escort her to her car. It wasn't far across the parking lot, in fact it was only a few steps in all, way too short for his taste.

She unlocked the car with a press of the key fob in her hand. The lights flickered as the locks clicked. "Thank you again for taking me out to the ranch. It was a lot of fun."

"You're welcome. I'm glad you enjoyed yourself."

"I did." She pressed her lips together as she dropped her gaze to the ground at their feet.

He stepped closer, bringing her head back up with a finger under her chin. The light from the street lamp illuminated her face. Her eyes sparkled in the light as her lips parted slightly. He couldn't stop himself from kissing her.

Their mouths met in the softest, barest touch. He lost himself in the feel of her lips as they molded to his. She sighed, allowing him access. Her hands were flat on his chest, but he could still feel her touch burning his skin through his shirt. His heart raced, pounding loudly in his ears. He rested his palms on her hips, bringing her closer to his body with a slight tug. He wanted to feel her molded to him as close as he could get.

A car honked as they went by, whistling loudly.

They separated reluctantly, but a smile lingered on her mouth when he looked down.

"Sorry about that."

"The kiss?"

"Oh hell no. The honking car. People are a bit redneck around here."

She giggled as she rested her forehead against his. He loved the way she did that.

"I should go," she whispered.

Her breath was warm against his mouth.

"I need to let you go."

"I wish I didn't have to."

"I know what you mean." He stepped back. "I'll see you tomorrow. Do you want to come out to the ranch in the morning? I know you need samples and stuff. I don't know if you need them specifically from our ground though."

She bit her lip for a moment before she smiled again. "I could use some from there even though I need a few more than just from there. That would be a good place to start. I can get some others from nearby too, while I'm out that way."

"Good. Maybe we could go for a ride."

"On a horse?"

"Well, sure."

"I've never been on a horse before."

"I'll teach you. It's easy. We have some real gentle ones that would be good for you. I've broke most every one of the horses on the ranch myself."

She nodded as she touched his face. He kissed her palm before it dropped to her side. "What time?"

"How about you come out for lunch at around eleven-thirty, and then we'll go out afterwards."

"All right."

He stepped back to give himself a little room to breathe. She tied him up in knots, and he really could use the air right now. "I'll see you tomorrow then."

"Yep."

"Good night, Rose."

"Good night, Joseph."

* * * *

Rose slipped into the driver's side of her rental car as Joseph pushed the door shut, tipped his hat, and then returned to his truck. A wistful sigh escaped her lips while she watched him in her side mirror. She touched the surface of her lips with her fingertips. They still tingled from his kiss.

She started the car, put it in drive, and pulled away from the curb. The hotel wasn't far, a few blocks down the road was all, but it gave her a little thrill to realize Joseph followed her to the hotel to make sure she got there okay.

He honked once before waving and turning around to head back down the road toward the ranch. Gentleman seemed to describe him to a T, and the thought of his little gestures made her heart trip over itself a little.

As she turned off the car and got ready to get out, her cell phone jingled in her purse. She grabbed it from its pocket in the back, turning it over to see who was calling.

Brandt.

She really needed to take his call.

"Hello?"

"Hey, sweetheart. How are things going in Texas?"

"Hi, Brandt." She gathered her thoughts for a moment. "Things are going fine here although I haven't been here long enough to really say much about it."

"I'm sure two days hasn't given you much time to do what you need to do yet."

"No, it hasn't. I've only settled into the hotel, unpacked my things and gotten something to eat." She cleared her throat knowing he was hinting at something. He always did. Now that she thought about it, his constant fishing for compliments and reassurance from her made him seem really annoying and not at all the self-assured man she'd originally thought he was.

"Do you miss me?"

She hesitated, realizing she really didn't miss him, not at all, but she couldn't tell him that. Brandt had been her constant companion for the last few years. They had dated for some time and had naturally gone to the next step with talking marriage. He considered himself her fiancé, although she didn't have a ring and he'd never really proposed. "Yes, of course I do." Her stomach knotted at the lie. She really wasn't an evil, conniving person but her spending time with Joseph felt like she was cheating.

"When will you be home, sweetheart?"

"Uh, I'm not sure, Brandt. It depends on how long it takes me to get the samples I need. I have to take them from several spots around the area, so it could take a week or more."

"How is the weather there?"

"Warm and sunny during the day, but not too hot yet. It's really nice."

"You sound like you are enjoying yourself." He sounded like a pouty five-year-old.

"I am for a change. Most of the time these trips are really boring. I've never been to Texas so it's a nice escape."

"But you love New York."

"I didn't say I didn't, Brandt. I like the area is all."

He went on for another several minutes talking about his work, his family, his apartment, his neighbors, and even his last meal.

"Listen, Brandt, I really need to go. I've been out all day and I'm exhausted. I just got back to my hotel room and I'm going to take a shower before I hit the bed."

"All right, sweetheart. I miss you and I can't wait for you to come home."

"I'll see you soon, I guess."

"I love you."

"Yeah, good night, Brandt." She hung up quickly before he could say another word. After spending the day with Joseph and his family, she realized that she wasn't in love with Brandt at all. Her idea of love was being with someone who could make her body tingle from a look, a touch of a hand that sent her heart to thundering in her chest, or the caress of a pair of lips that made her want to tear clothes off and do naughty things.

She blew out a breath, pushed open her car door, and climbed out.

The night sky was brilliantly lit with stars. Her head back, she stared at the beautiful sight above her head. *They've never looked this bright in New York.*

After a moment, she pulled out her room key, shut the door on the car, and walked to her room. She glanced across the road to where The Dusty Boot sat. Music blared as the doors opened and closed with each patron that moved through them. Men and women alike stood outside, some smoking cigarettes, and some hanging around talking with others. Everyone was dressed in jeans, western shirts, cowboy boots, and hats, even the women. A few men good-naturedly shoved each other as laughter echoed through the night, reaching her on the breeze.

The building itself caught her eye. A huge neon boot blinked over the top of the building. There was even a wooden rail along the sidewalk that reminded her of some old western movie where they tied their horses. Bright beer signs blinked in the windows advertising different types of the malt liquor for the patrons to try.

She smiled when she thought about Joseph taking her there tomorrow night. Shivering in the cooling night air, she wondered if it was from the weather or the anticipation of tomorrow. Her phone beeping brought her back to the present and Brandt's call. She blew out a frustrated breath. Better to deal with these feelings than let herself get any more bitter toward him than she already was.

Things with him hadn't been that great the last few weeks before she left. He'd become needy and clinging. He'd started asking her to do things for him like pick up his dry cleaning, do his grocery shopping, and he'd even asked her to buy his mother an anniversary gift, from him of course.

Lately, she'd even been going over to his house to pick up after him, make his bed, hang up his clothes, clean his apartment, and water his plants.

God forbid, she say anything about their sex life. Not that it had ever been much to talk about. He wasn't inventive in the bedroom and if she suggested anything new, he would say something about where she'd heard of that or had she been talking to her friends about what they did in the bedroom. It was straight missionary for him and most of the time it was over in a matter of minutes, leaving her unsatisfied. She had a feeling sex with Joseph wouldn't be boring in any sense of the word.

With a tired sigh, she headed for her room and slipped the key into the lock. The simple room was clean and simply adorned without much luxury outside of the bed, a dresser with an older television set sitting on top, and a small table with a chair for working on her computer. The clean but faded coverlet on the bed was typical for a hotel room with bright swirls and a paisley design. The curtains on the window were the same pattern. The bathroom was small, but it had a nice tub and shower combination that had a great showerhead in it.

She laid her purse on the table, kicked off her shoes, and sat down on the edge of the bed. She needed to get up, get her comfy PJs on and go to bed, but she felt wound up. Spending the day on the ranch seemed to have done that to her. She didn't really feel all that sleepy even though she really should be exhausted from all the excitement.

She tapped her fingers on her lips as she thought about what she could do to unwind. *Maybe a hot bath would be good or a nice novel to read. I have one of Mesa's books in my carryon that I was reading on the plane.*

With a smile of anticipation on her lips, she stood and grabbed her carryon bag from the floor next to the dresser. She pulled the paperback from the bag and turned it over in her hand to read the back.

What happens when a city girl meets a real hometown cowboy from a small town in Texas?

Sparks fly.

Missy Anderson leaves her comfortable existence in the big city to see what life might hold in Texas where the Bluebonnets bloom, everything is much simpler, summers are hot, and the men are hotter. When she's almost run over by a muddy, jacked up four-by-four and literally knocked on her butt by a handsome cowboy, she isn't prepared for the crystal clear blue eyes staring back. No one told her a cowboy might bowl her over with his gentlemanly behavior, sexy dimpled smile, and gorgeous ass in those jeans.

Dalton Jameson is as cowboy as they come. Born and raised on a small Texas ranch, he'd been breaking horses, riding fences, branding cattle, and living the cowboy dream since the day he'd been old enough to straddle a horse. Life didn't come better than waking up to a beautiful sunrise with a cup of coffee in his left hand and a set of reins in his right. The only thing missing was a cowgirl to call his own. He'd never pictured her as a woman with bright red hair, big green eyes, brand new cowboy boots, tight bespangled jeans, with an equally flashy blouse who he'd landed on when she almost got run over in the middle of town.

Can a woman who is used to catered meals, fancy cars, and diamonds and pearls be interested in a guy who drives a tractor, rides horses, and goes two-steppin' on Saturday nights? Can two such different people find what they are yearning for in the arms of a stranger?

She sighed as she hugged the book to her chest. Mesa's books had touched her in ways she hadn't even been aware of until recently. They made her lose herself in the story, picturing her own hair flying behind her as she rode across hills and valleys beside a gorgeous man on horseback. It didn't matter that she'd never ridden one before. She could still almost feel the soreness between her legs after she'd dismounted.

What about how her heroes made love? Holy shit, she wanted that, wanted it so badly she could almost taste it on her tongue. The excitement of making love with a man who knew what he was doing and cared about her satisfaction would be phenomenal. Brandt had always taken his pleasure, never caring whether she'd had an orgasm or not. In fact, most of the time she had to wait until he went to sleep, and then masturbated herself to one to get anything out of their sexual encounters.

A deep sigh escaped her at understanding how pathetic her relationship with Brandt actually was. He definitely wasn't the man she wanted to spend the rest of her life with anymore.

She licked her lips realizing she could still taste Joseph on them. Her heart did a little happy beat in her chest when she thought about experiencing a little more with him.

A breakup with Brandt was in order before she could give into those fantasies though.

Chapter Six

Joey cracked open his eyelids to the sunshine coming through the window of his room. When he rolled over the clock on the bedside table read six. He groaned softly as he buried his head under the pillow.

Sleep hadn't come easy for him the night before. Fanciful thoughts of one red haired girl had plagued him all night. Dreams of making love to her over and over had made it too uncomfortable to sleep. They kept dissipating the minute he'd be ready to bury himself in her sweet heat, leaving him aching and horny. His cock was already hard this morning.

He groaned as he rolled out from under the covers. Work called, much to his chagrin. He had horses to feed, stalls to clean, and tack to clean. His work day began early and didn't let up until the sun went down, but tonight he had a date, a date with a gorgeous woman that he couldn't seem to get out of his head.

Shower first, then work.

He grabbed a clean set of clothes and headed for the bathroom. It wasn't much since his room was one of the cabins farther away from the main lodge. He liked having his own space even though it didn't consist of a lot. A big room for his personal things like his bed, his dresser, his television, a computer, and a closet for his clothes was all he needed. The bathroom was separate and only had a bath/shower combination, a sink, and a toilet. It was enough for now. He didn't need much since he didn't have a woman and a bunch of kids like his brothers. When it was time for him to build his house, he'd have it on his piece of land his parents gave him on his eighteenth birthday.

The acreage was perfect with its own little pond, a great place for the house, and some land for him to raise horses.

He turned on the shower, letting it run for a few minutes to get some hot water going before he climbed inside. Once he stood underneath the spray, he let the water run over his head, sluicing down his chest in long rivulets. His thoughts drifted off to the beautiful redhead he'd met yesterday and what it would feel like to have her on her knees in the shower with him, sucking his cock like she wanted nothing more than to bring him to a shouting orgasm.

Deciding not to fight the fantasy, he palmed his cock with his right hand as he placed his left on the tile wall. He could picture her so clearly, gazing up at him with those emerald green eyes, her gorgeous long hair trailing down her back in long waves. Her lips parted as she smiled up at him, took him in her hand, and ran her tongue from the base of his cock to the tip. As her mouth engulfed the head of his cock, he groaned deep in his throat. The wet, warm sensations had him on the edge of climax within minutes, but he didn't want to come so soon. He wanted to relish her hot mouth around him. He dropped his head back on his shoulders as she continued to suck him until his legs shook.

Taking his balls in her hands, she rolled the flesh in her palm and continued to run her tongue up and around his cock. His pleasure reaching its climax, he grabbed her hair in his fists, guiding her to what would bring him to the brink of ecstasy.

His balls drew up against his groin as his orgasm hovered right on the precipice.

Seconds later, cum shot out of the end of his dick, painting the tile wall in front of him. A moan escaped his lips as he collapsed against the cold tile. "Fuck."

His breath came out in rapid pants as he tried to get his body under control. It had been a long time since he'd come that hard.

After he recovered, he grabbed the soap, washed the speckles of cum from his abdomen, and scrubbed the rest of his body clean. Shampoo came next as he scrubbed his hair.

He turned the water off after rinsing all the soap away and then grabbed a towel from the rack. Once he was dry, he pulled on his clean clothes, combed out his hair, put on some deodorant, and headed back into the bedroom to tug on his boots.

Coffee would definitely be required this morning. Maybe a bucketful of pure caffeine to keep him functioning.

The table by the door held his keys, his wallet, his cell phone, and his sunglasses in a small bowl. He slid everything into his pockets, except his sunglasses, which went on his face. Grabbing his hat off the rack on the wall, he placed it on his head.

When he opened the door, he was hit by a blast of cooler air. Apparently spring wasn't ready to give way to the warmer temperatures of Texas just yet. *It couldn't be much warmer than about forty degrees today.* Deciding to take his jacket with him, he grabbed it off the hook and slipped it on. The barn would be cold this morning.

He pulled the door shut behind him before he jiggled the handle to make sure it was locked. Even though there wasn't much worry about anyone on the place stealing things, he didn't want to tempt fate. Last summer they'd had a guest steal a few items before he'd been caught by Jason and escorted off the property.

His steps took him across the ground via the relatively long concrete walkway to the main lodge where coffee would be brewing. Those who worked the kitchen would be there already getting things ready for the guests' breakfast.

Since they had such a large crowd right now, breakfast would be a big deal. Mesa's romance writer friends would be going home soon, but for now, they were guests and thus treated with every convenience the ranch could muster. It was kind of nice having a large group on the ranch during what was usually a slow period. They'd been really fun to have around these last few days.

Joey rounded the front of the main lodge and stopped dead in his tracks. Sitting in one of the chairs in front of the window was the old cowboy they'd seen over and over on the ranch since they'd lived there. They didn't know who he was but he showed himself sometimes at the oddest times.

The old man nodded, smiled, and then faded away like the morning mist.

Joey had always been fascinated by the stories of the ghosts on the ranch and now that he had a little time, he thought he might do some research on the place. It would be kind of cool if he could find out who the old man was. He knew the place had been a working brothel way back when, but it had also been a working ranch for many years. The old cowboy was probably a ranch hand who loved the place so much, he couldn't leave, even in death.

After a moment, he shook his head and continued on down the front porch to check on the donkeys before he went inside for his coffee. The donkey family they had were great for the guests. They liked being petted and fed when the guests were around, so they were real friendly, but it was his job as the head wrangler to make sure they were clean, trimmed, and in good shape.

He rounded the far corner of the porch to find the donkeys happily munching on some new spring grass. "There you are."

They jerked their heads up, ears forward, and started toward him. They knew who took care of them.

"Come on, Jack, Jenny, and Junior. I need to trim your hooves today so that means going to the barn."

The donkey family happily followed him out around the back of the main lodge, across the parking lot for the guests' cars, and to the barn in the distance. He would get them into a stall with some sweet feed, lock the door, and then get his coffee. It could get interesting rounding those three up in the mornings.

Once he got them locked in a stall, he headed back to the big house to grab his coffee and maybe a muffin to tie him over until breakfast was ready.

He pushed open the side door of the main lodge and moved inside. Scents of baking reached his nose, making his stomach growl in anticipation of a warm blueberry muffin. The coffee pot sat on the table near where the family usually ate their meals, ready and waiting with its luminescent red light on telling him that it was ready and hot. Finding his normal cup sitting in the clean rack, he grabbed it and stuck it under the spout before pulling the handle down to fill the cup. After he doctored it with a little cream and sugar, he sipped on the hot liquid as he groaned in appreciation.

"Mornin', Joey."

He turned to find Jonathan's girl, Mandy, walking toward him with muffins in a basket. "Mornin', Mandy. Are there blueberry in there?"

"Of course. I know how you love those and it's your early day in the barn this morning."

"God love you, woman." He kissed her on the cheek.

"You are such a sweetheart. I hope you find a nice girl soon, and that doesn't mean that little slut next door."

He frowned as he mumbled through the muffin. "Jessie?"

"Yeah, that's her." She nodded. "Be careful of her. She's out to trap her a Young brother and you're the only one left."

"Don't worry, Mandy."

Mandy laid the basket of muffins on the table near the coffee pot. "I think that girl you brought to dinner last night was cute. You met her at the diner?"

"Yes. She was sketching at one of the tables." He shoved another bite of muffin into his mouth. "She's really good."

"She doesn't live here?"

"No. She's from New York."

"What's she doing in Bandera, Texas?"

"She's a microbiologist. She's here to study the water and soil for the company she works for."

Mandy's brow crinkled as she frowned. "Okay."

Joseph laughed. "I don't know much about it either. I'm only a simple cowboy." Mandy punched him in the arm as he faked being hurt while he rubbed his bicep. "Ow!"

"Yeah, whatever, you ass. You have more talent in your pinky than most of the men on this place. You have a way with animals they could only hope to have."

He shrugged, dropping his gaze to the floor. "I ain't nothin' special."

She pushed his hat back. "You are too. You single-handedly run that barn with all those horses for the guests, break new animals that come in, keep the donkey family happy, and most importantly you keep the horses taken care of so they can give the guests the cowboy experience they are here for. You are very special."

"Okay, okay. Thanks for the pep talk."

"You're welcome. Now, I'm sure you have some hungry animals out there to take care of. I can hear the donkeys braying all the way up here."

"Yeah, they weren't happy to be locked in the stall."

"They never are, but they need to be taken care of too. All the crap they get from the dining room can't be good for them."

He leaned in a kissed her on the cheek again. "You are a special woman, Mandy."

They could hear a pair of boots on the hardwood as Jonathan appeared around the corner of the dining room. "You bet she is, brother, now get your hands off my lady."

Joseph grinned as he turned on his booted heels and headed back for the barn. He was glad Jonathan finally came to his senses about Mandy. She'd been a part of the group at Thunder Ridge for a few years now. Her pining over his brother had been apparent to everyone but him. Jonathan had realized if he didn't do something soon, he'd lose his chance with the feisty blonde. They were planning to get married soon.

He frowned as his boots crunched under the gravel of the walkway. All of his brothers were paired off now, leaving him to fend for himself when it came to women. He really didn't think he was ready to settle down yet. He still had a lot of living to do, and besides, he wasn't financially prepared to take on a wife. He didn't have much in savings except for a few thousand he'd managed to squirrel away from riding broncs on the rodeo circuit.

As he passed through the big double doors of the barn, he was surrounded by familiar scents. The mixed aromas of horses, hay, manure, and leather met his nose, making him smile. The smells embraced him as he inhaled a big deep breath. Home.

A soft whistle left his lips as he walked down the dirt center of the barn toward his small office space in the back. He kept his records and such in there, so he knew exactly when each horse was born, broke, died, retired or foaled. It was important for him to know these facts since he was responsible for every animal on the place.

Today meant a trip into town too. He needed to get the feed and get the mare broke he'd forgotten about yesterday, not that he'd minded being distracted. The pretty redhead was quite the distraction.

Excitement rippled down his back when he thought about her. He glanced at his watch. Still too early for her to be here. He'd told her eleven. He snapped his figures. *I'll trim the donkeys, run into town for feed, and be back in time for her to be here for lunch.*

He nodded at his plan as he grabbed his snippers and file before he went back down to the stall he'd locked the donkeys in. Jack kicked the door as he approached. "Easy, boy. I'm comin'."

When he reached the stall, he popped open the door and stepped inside to hook a lead rope to the donkey's halter. He led him out into the middle of the walkway, shutting the door behind him so Jenny and Junior wouldn't come out. They had hooks connected to two of the wooden beams in order to saddle horses, work on them, or whatever they needed to do. Once he had Jack crosstied, he went back down the aisle to where he'd hung his leather chaps. He needed those to keep his legs safe in case something went terribly wrong while he was shoeing or clipping hooves. Lucky for him, he hadn't had a problem in a long time.

The chaps around his hips and legs, he got the nippers out, picked up a hoof and started trimming around it. Jack was a patient animal, always standing perfectly still while he did what he had to do. Jenny wasn't such an easy one to work on and forget Junior. Being so young, the little guy needed some help being comfortable with getting his feet trimmed.

He worked for over an hour on the three donkeys, getting them brushed, feet trimmed and ready to meet their public. He laughed to himself. The donkeys had a fan club even.

By the time he was done, it was almost time for breakfast. He would have to hurry if he was going to get the horses fed, watered and saddled for the nine o'clock trail ride and be inside for his own food. He hated missing breakfast.

Jeff drove up in his truck, parking near the barn. He got out and walked through the double doors. "Need some help?"

"Yeah, a little. I trimmed hooves this morning and got a little behind. If you can get the horses out and fill their water buckets, I'll get the feed. Is anyone else around who might be able to saddle some of them?"

"I think Joel is inside. Let me go see if I can find him."

"Thanks."

"Sure."

Jeff disappeared for several minutes into the main lodge, but when he returned he had Joel and Jason with him. "These two were hanging out near the coffee pot."

Joseph laughed before he started directing everyone to what he needed done. Within thirty minutes, they had all the horses being used that day tied out in their spots in the corral, watered, fed, and saddled. "Thanks, guys."

"You're welcome. Now you don't have to miss breakfast." Joel laughed as he slapped Joey on the back. "I know how irritable you can get without food."

"Asshole."

Joel grinned as they all headed toward the house just as the breakfast bell began to clang, calling everyone in for the meal.

Breakfast was the social event of the hour at the ranch. Most of the guests made it to the first meal of the day before they went on with the other activities available at the ranch. It was still rather cool outside in the mornings, so there wouldn't be anyone swimming, and since the majority of the guests on the ranch at the moment were Mesa's writer friends, much of their time seemed to be spent observing the guys.

The room buzzed with conversation as they headed toward the family table. A couple of women whistled when they walked by. Joel tipped his hat and grinned the patent Young grin, leaving them laughing behind him.

"Mesa, you got so lucky, girl. I want me a cowboy."

Mesa wrapped her arms around Joel's shoulders and kissed him on the mouth. "Well, there is only of the boys not attached. Keep your hands off Joel. He's mine."

"You bet, babe." He swept her up in a hug, twirling her around a couple of times as the women behind them sighed.

"Point out the one that isn't taken."

"Come up here, Joey."

She motioned at him with her hand as he tried to blend into the woodwork. Leave it to Mesa to embarrass the hell of out him. She knew he didn't like to be the center of attention, except in the rodeo arena. He shook his head.

She grabbed his hand and dragged him out in front of everyone. He could feel his face flush beet red.

"This, ladies, is Joseph Young. He's the youngest of the boys. He's the head wrangler on the place. He likes working with his hands, rope, leather, and occasionally rides rodeo. He stands over six feet tall and built solid. Wouldn't you love running your hands over these muscles?"

He was going to kill her even if she was his sister-in-law. "Mesa," he growled.

"He growls too, ladies."

The women twittered behind their hands.

"I'm going to sit down."

Mesa laughed as he turned his back to the group and walked to the family table. "And look at that butt in those jeans!"

He stopped next to Joel. "I'm going to kill your wife."

"She's only havin' fun at your expense."

"I realize that, but I'm still going to kill her because now they won't leave me alone for the rest of the time they're here."

"They might if you bring that pretty redhead back."

"She'll be here for lunch."

Joel grinned and slapped him on the back. "She seems to like you."

"I like her too."

"Better than Jessie?"

He thought about that for a moment and realized yeah, he liked Rose a lot more than he liked Jessica or any other woman he'd known in his past. "Yeah. I guess I do."

"You are a goner, buddy."

A few hours later, after he'd made the run into town for feed and Jeff, Joel, and Jason helped him unload, he paced the walkway from the barn to the back of the cabins as he waited for Rose to appear. The anxiousness sitting in the pit of his stomach worried him. He wasn't used to being this way with a woman, any woman. It wasn't like there could be anything between them anyway. She didn't live here. Hell, she lived at least a couple of thousand miles away.

He stopped in the doorway of the barn and turned to watch the driveway. He took off his hat and ran his fingers through his hair before putting it back on his head. Why he was so nervous about seeing her again, he wasn't sure. Yeah, she was pretty, smart, and all that, but it was something more, something he wasn't sure he wanted to explore.

The gate was too far away to see, but when a cloud of dust appeared, he moved toward the parking lot to await her arrival. He glanced at his watch, right on time. It was unheard of for any woman he knew to be punctual, apparently she was an exception to the rule.

When she stopped the car near the bottom of the hill by the pool, he hurried his steps to reach her side before she had a chance to get out of the car. He pulled open the door, grinning as she let out a startled squeak. "I didn't mean to frighten you."

"Joseph." She sighed. "I didn't expect you to be right here by the car. I'm sure you have work to do, right?"

"True, but I've been waiting for you."

"I'm flattered," she said, stepping out and pushing the door shut behind her. "Have you been busy this morning?"

"Yeah, a little. Nothing too strenuous though. I trimmed the donkeys, got the horses being used today ready to ride, normal stuff." He placed his hand at the small of her back to lead her toward the house. "Lunch should be ready shortly."

She giggled as they walked. "I'm going to get fat with all this food you have around here."

"You? No way. Besides, we have a lot of things you can do around here to work off whatever you eat."

"Oh?"

His thoughts went straight into the toilet as he imagined her spread out on a bale of hay waiting for him with her arms raised above her head, her red hair spread out around her like a halo, and a come-hither smile on her lips. "Yeah." He'd had women in the barn before, on a few occasions, but he couldn't get the thought of Rose in the hayloft with him out of his head. He cleared his throat trying to dispel the image. "I've talked to Mesa, and she would love to meet you."

"Really?"

"Yeah. She likes meeting her fans."

"I wish I had all my books with me. I have several of hers, but I only brought one."

"I'm sure she'd be glad to sign it."

She placed her hand on his arm to stop his steps. "Thank you, Joseph."

When her lips brushed his cheek, he had to keep himself from grabbing her, pulling her into his arms, and devouring her mouth.

As she stepped back, he took her hand, threaded their fingers together, and continued onto the main lodge. "There may be some other authors here that you know. Most of them are western authors from what I understand. I don't know if you read those or not."

"I've read some, yes, but I feel very ignorant when it comes to horses and stuff."

"I think the authors are going home on Monday, so you have a few days if you want to talk to them."

A frown pulled down the corners of her mouth. "I don't want to ruin my time with you either. I think you are a very special person, and I'm enjoying your company."

"I like having you here."

She smiled again as he opened the door for her to go in front of him. When they walked inside, the room was in total chaos as it had been since this group had arrived. They spent every waking moment in the main lodge or outside with his brothers, writing things down, taking pictures, and doing whatever it is writers do. He had to laugh a little because they were a nosy bunch.

One of the authors got up from her seat and came toward them, stopping them in the middle of walkway. "Hi, Joseph."

"Hello."

She ran a finger down his chest. "I could really use some personal, one-on-one time with you. You know, for research."

"Uh, sorry, but I have a friend here today that I'm helping with a project."

The woman glanced at Rose before focusing on him again. "Are you going to be busy all weekend?"

"Probably." *God, I hope so. This woman is at least twenty years older than me.* "I'm sorry. We appreciate you coming to the ranch, but Rose needs my help with gathering some samples from our property. I'm sure it will take until at least Tuesday." He glanced down into Rose's eyes. "Right, Rose?" *I hope she gets my message.*

"Yes, of course. Tuesday will probably be the soonest we are finished."

"I'm sure you understand."

The woman fingered the buttons on the front of his shirt. Apprehension slithered down his spine as he grasped Rose's hand tighter. When the woman looked up, he caught something in her gaze that he wasn't sure he liked. Determination to get what she wanted, stared back.

"All right then. Maybe some other time."

"Sure."

She stepped away and went back to her spot near her friends, but her gaze never left his back as he continued toward the family table with Rose by his side.

"I don't trust her," Rose whispered as he pulled out the chair for her.

"Yeah, me either, but it is what it is. I'll keep a close eye on her."

"Do you always get that kind of attention?"

"More and more these days."

"Why is that? I mean other than you being a very handsome man."

He smiled as he looked down into her eyes. "Thank you, but it's mostly because I'm the only unattached cowboy left of the original nine brothers. It comes with its hazards, I guess." He pulled up the chair next to her and sat down. "We have to be nice to the guests, so it comes with getting attention we might not necessarily want."

"I see."

He took her hand in his, slowly rubbing a spot on the back. He liked the feeling of her skin beneath his. It was very soft to the touch. "I don't worry much about them. They'll be gone soon."

Mesa walked over from where she'd been sitting with a small group at one of the large square tables. "You must be Rose."

"I...yes."

Mesa held out her hand. "I'm Mesa Young or Mesa West is how you might know me."

Rose put her hand to her throat and stuttered out a few words that made no sense to him at all.

"It's okay. I just wanted to stop and say hello. I hear you like my books."

"Yes, ma'am. I love them. I have your latest in my hotel room. I'm reading it right now."

"Thank you, Rose. I appreciate you being a fan, and I hope you are enjoying the book."

"Tremendously." Rose leaned toward Mesa slightly. "Tell me. Are your cowboys based on Joel and his brothers?"

Mesa laughed. "Some, yes, but not always. The boys are great inspiration though." Mesa laid her hand on his shoulder. "In fact, the one I'm currently writing reminds me a lot of Joey."

"Really?"

"Yes, but don't tell him that. He might get a big head or something." She leaned down and kissed him on the cheek. "Love you, Joey."

"Love you too, Mesa, now go back over there and behave or I'll have Joel take a switch to your behind."

Mesa's eyes widened as a grin spread across her lips. "I might like it."

"You just might."

When Mesa walked away, Rose turned to him and whispered under her breath, "Do you like to spank women?"

Chapter Seven

Joseph coughed and sputtered as his eyes widened. "Well, I, uh…"

"I'm kidding, Joseph." She giggled before laying her hand on his thigh. "Whatever you do in the bedroom is your business."

He smiled and touched her nose with his finger.

A sigh escaped her lips when he stood so they could get their lunch since the guests had already retrieved theirs. As she followed him to the line, he pushed her in front of him, giving her the opportunity to get her food first.

"Guests first."

"I'm not a guest."

"Yes, you are. You're my guest."

He put his hands on her hips and turned her so her back was to his chest. Shivers raced down her spine as she felt his warm breath on her neck where she'd tied her hair up in a ponytail today. She wanted his lips there more than anything she could think of. Her feet felt like lead when she took a step toward the food being served. *How fast can this meal be over?*

Her thoughts did a one-eighty when she remembered Brandt. She'd been so inspired by Mesa's book that dealing with the reality of her own relationship slipped her mind this morning. *Well shit. I need to take care of that pronto, otherwise, I can't move forward with Joseph even if it's a temporary thing.*

Do I want to end things with Brandt if this thing with Joseph is only for a few weeks?

Yes.

After lunch I will take a moment and call Brandt to cut things off.

"You okay?" he asked as they took their seats and he set her plate down in front of her.

"I'm fine. I just remembered I need to make a phone call after we are done eating."

"Sure." He glanced down at her and then to the refreshment table. "Tea, lemonade, or water?"

"Lemonade would be great. Thank you."

As the rest of the family returned to the table, conversation flowed around her. She couldn't quite keep up with what everyone was talking about, so she focused on one conversation near her between Jackson and Samantha.

"Babe, we need to work on the tour schedule this afternoon."

"I need to rehearse this afternoon, Jackson. The guys from the band are traveling into San Antonio so we can work on some new material."

"I realize that, but I can't book your dates if I don't know what we already have in the pipeline."

Samantha wiped something from the corner of his mouth. "It will work out, cowboy. It always does." She leaned in a kissed him on the mouth.

Rose sighed as she watched. She wanted that more than anything. She wanted to be able to touch a guy tenderly, stroke his skin, run her fingers through his hair, and be with him every moment without worrying about how uncomfortable that made him feel. Couples shouldn't be uncomfortable around each other like her and Brandt had become. He didn't like when she watched television while he was working on paperwork. He didn't like what she cooked for dinner. He didn't like how she did his laundry. He didn't like how she wanted more from their sex life. *Why haven't I broken up with him before now?*

What appeared to be an argument coming to a head at the end of the table caught her attention.

"No, Jason."

"Now, Peyton, you know you want to."

"No, actually, I don't. We've had this discussion." Peyton glanced around the table, lowering her voice, but not enough that Rose couldn't hear it. "Stop badgering me. I'm not going to change my mind."

"Why? I don't understand."

"We are not having this conversation at the family table, Jason. I've told you where I stand on this subject, we've talked about it, and you said you understood. Are you saying now you don't?"

"Baby, I know you are apprehensive, but it's a natural thing. It's what couples do when they are married and in love."

"This half of this couple doesn't want any."

Nina laid her napkin aside and focused on Peyton. "Is everything all right, Peyton?"

"You know what, no, it's not. Jason and I have had a conversation about having children. I don't want any, period. He's being persistent that I will change my mind once I become pregnant. He said he understood, but now he's driving me nuts with all this talk about babies."

"Jason, why don't you and Peyton take this into the office," Nina suggested as she glanced at the now quiet room.

"Fine." Jason grabbed his wife's hand, pulled her up, and dragged her off down the hall and around the corner until they disappeared from view.

A door slammed in the distance.

Rose swallowed hard as she glanced at Joseph.

Nina rose from her seat to address the group in the dining room. "Sorry. That shouldn't have happened at the table. We try to encourage our children to talk out their problems, but we do hope they won't do it in front of guests. Please accept our apologies and enjoy the rest of your meal."

Lunch continued as a quiet affair and Rose couldn't wait to leave. Couple problems always made her anxious whether they were her own or someone else's.

When they'd finished their meal, Joseph grabbed their plates to put them in the dish bin.

"Ready to go?"

"Yes." She breathed a sigh of relief to be able to go outside into the sunshine and forget the tension in the room.

He held open the door as she passed through it and then placed his palm at the small of her back to guide her toward the barn.

As they moved through the huge doorway into the cooler interior of the barn, her eyes adjusted to the dark and she noticed several horses still in their stalls. She knew Joseph would have already taken several out to have them ready for guests to ride. She couldn't wait to get on the back of a horse. Ever since she was a little girl, she'd wanted a horse.

"Uh, can you give me a few minutes to make that call I mentioned?"

"Sure. You can use Jeremiah's office, if you want. He's still in the house with Callie, so he won't disturb you."

"Thank you. Are we going riding today?"

"If you want, but first I need to teach you a few things about being around horses. After you make your call, we can grab the tack for them. I didn't saddle my horse this morning and the one you would ride isn't saddled either."

"Okay." She loved the smell of the tack room. When they'd been in there before, she pulled all those scents into her lungs and held them. Leather had always turned her on.

They passed through the doorway and Joseph moved toward where the saddles were kept on the wall. She went to the open door to Jeremiah's office and closed it behind her as she pulled out her cell phone.

"Hello?"

"Hi, Brandt."

"Hi, Rose. It's odd for you to be calling me in the middle of the day. Is there something wrong?"

"No. You aren't in a meeting, are you?"

"No. I'm free for about thirty minutes. I have a client coming in for a consultation after lunch."

"Oh. I forgot that Texas is an hour behind New York."

"Is something wrong, honey?"

"Listen, Brandt. I know things have not been great between us for some time. We've been drifting apart for months, you don't like how I do many of the things around our place, and face it, sex between us has gotten to the point where it's boring."

"What are you saying, Rose?"

"I don't want to see you anymore. I will have my father come over and move my personal things out of our apartment tomorrow. The rest of my furniture and bigger items will be taken care of when I get back from Texas in a week or so."

"What!"

"I'm sorry, Brandt, but I feel this is for the best. I'm not in love with you anymore and I think the best thing for us both is to move on."

"What the hell, Rose? Are you seeing some hick Texas cowboy or something? Where did this come from? Everything was fine before you left."

"No, no it wasn't, Brandt. Things have been bad for me for a while. And no, I'm not seeing some hick Texas cowboy while I'm here. I've made a few friends, but that's it. I'm trying to get my work done so I can come back to New York, but I don't want to come back to you."

"You can't do this! I had plans for us, big plans. I need you by my side when I make partner at the firm. I need your father's backing."

"Excuse me?"

"You heard me. I need your father's backing, his financial support while I'm working on making partner and when I start my political career. You owe me!"

"For one, neither I, nor my father, owe you anything, Brandt. Apparently, you've been after my family's financial backing all this time, and I just wasn't aware of your motivation. Now that I am, I don't feel the least bit sorry to be ending this relationship. As I said, I will have my father come over tomorrow to pack my personal items. If they aren't in pristine condition when he arrives, you will be hearing from my attorney. Since both of our names are on the lease, I will be contacting the landlord to let them know you will be staying, but I'm leaving. We are already past our lease date on this apartment, so me moving out shouldn't be a problem with them."

"You can't do this, Rose! I love you. I need you. Don't walk out on me, please."

His whiny voice grated on her nerves as she held the phone away from her ear. "I'm done, Brandt. I'm sorry it has to end this way, but I need to try new things and staying with you isn't in the cards. Goodbye." She hit the end button on her cell and exhaled a long, slow breath. *That wasn't pleasant at all.*

Checking her appearance, she looked down at her blouse tucked into her brand new jeans and saw the dust on the tips of her brand new cowboy boots. At least Joseph couldn't say she hadn't dressed the part today. Feeling relieved and a little more lighthearted, she pushed open the door and came face to face with a scowling Joseph Young.

"Joseph? Is there a problem?"

"Why didn't you tell me you had a boyfriend, Rose? You let me kiss you by the pond." His hat hit the floor behind him as he raked his fingers through his hair. "What the hell?"

"That's not it at all."

"What is it then, Rose? I don't mess with women who belong to someone else." He reached down and picked up his hat before shoving it back on his head.

Irritation radiated off him in waves.

She moved close enough to touch him as she reached up and smoothed the frown lines from his face. "I assume you heard part of my conversation."

"Yeah."

"I did have a boyfriend when I came here. His name is Brandt and he's an attorney."

"Fucking wonderful." He spun on his heel and moved toward one of the stalls.

He pulled back his arm and punched his hand through the board in front of him. When he lifted his hand to his face, his knuckles were bleeding and torn.

She winced as she touched his back, smoothing his shirt over his broad shoulders. "Joseph, I'm sorry. I never meant to hurt you." She put her forehead on his shoulder blade. "When you kissed me the first time, it was like I awoke from a dream. It was so different from anything I'd experienced." He hadn't moved. Hell, she wasn't sure he'd heard her except for the pounding of his heart under her cheek when she laid it flat on his back and encircled his waist with her arms. "I broke up with him on the phone. Things haven't been good between us for a long time. You made me see that. You brought out sensations in me I've never felt with him and it made me realize things with him were bad for a while."

"Maybe you shouldn't have broken up with him. Maybe you should have tried to work things out." He turned to face her and she was taken aback by the look in his eyes. Frustration, anger, and disappointment reflected in his gaze.

She touched his face. "I'm attracted to you, which is why I broke things off with him. I didn't feel it was fair to either of you to be playing like that." After several tense moments, he framed her face with his hands, grimacing when he bent his knuckles. "You should clean that up," she whispered, her gaze stopping on his lips and how close they were to her mouth. She wanted his mouth on hers. She needed to feel his lips brushing hers, his tongue demanding entrance, and his body wrapped around hers. The passion between them could set the barn on fire, if they let it, but he was holding back.

She looked up into his eyes. The brown of his irises looked like dark chocolate. She wanted to drown in him.

"Joseph," she murmured, drawing his gaze to her lips.

"Why do I feel like I'm drowning in your eyes? I can't help myself when I'm around you. I have this desperate need to touch you, kiss you, and see what making love to you would be like." He continued to stare at her face, his gaze running over the surfaces for long moments before he slowly brought their mouths together. The soft meeting of their lips, the feel of his hands framing her face, and the warmth of his body close to hers had her sighing into his mouth. Being kissed like this, so softly and so gently, was something she'd only ever dreamed of. The man knew how to kiss.

Tingling started in her toes and rushed up her legs as if her feet had gone to sleep. Her whole body turned warm and languid, pliable to his hands. The need for something to anchor her had her wrapping her hands around his wrists as her body came alive under his. Her nipples pulled into tight little nubs. Her belly turned into one large knot as she waited for him to do something, anything.

His tongue slipped along the seam of her lips, asking for permission to take the kiss deeper. When she opened her mouth, a growl erupted from him as he tilted his head and devoured her. It was the only word she could think of for the way he ate at her mouth, his tongue sliding over hers in a desperate need to taste her, kiss her, and make her his.

His hands wandered over her shoulders, and down her arms, stopping at her waist. He grasped her hips and pulled her into his embrace so they were touching from lips to hips. His cock lay hard against her belly, clearly outlined by his jeans.

When his lips left hers, he kissed his way across her cheek, nibbling along her jawline with his teeth as she tipped her head back to give him better access to what he desired. One hand came up to cup her breast, rasping his thumb across the already hard nipple.

"God, Joseph."

He growled low in his throat as he snuck his hand up her blouse.

Skin to skin felt amazing. The calluses on his hand rubbed deliciously against her flesh. She wrapped her arms around his shoulders, giving him better access to her breast. When his hand pushed her bra out of the way, she sucked in a ragged breath as a shiver raced down her spine. The callus on his thumb scraped the tip of her nipple, driving a moan from her mouth.

His hand grasped the ponytail holder and pulled it out of her hair, leaving it flowing down around her shoulders. He lifted his head, looking down into her gaze. "I love your hair," he whispered before he buried his hands in the strands, pulling her head back again. "It works so well when I want your neck bared to my touch."

He nipped at her neck as he worked his way from her jaw to her collarbone. The little bites on her flesh drove her wild with desire. Brandt had never taken what he wanted when they made love. She had a feeling Joseph would give her little choice as he played her body until she was strung tighter than a violin string.

His breath came out in rasping pants against her skin as he slowed down, touching her softly before he removed his hands altogether and stepped back.

Fog clouded her brain as she tried to figure out why he stopped. "Joseph?"

"Rose, you are so beautiful, so sexy." He kissed her nose. "God, I want you so bad, I hurt, but I don't want to take something you aren't willing to give me. Your body is something precious. Making love with you would be very special to me, but we haven't known each other very long, only a couple of days, and I don't want to take advantage of you." He turned his back and walked a few steps away from her, lacing his hands behind his head.

She pressed herself against his back. "You won't be taking advantage of me. I want you to make love to me. I want to feel what it's like to be with someone who takes care of my needs. I think you would be that guy."

"You know I can't promise anything beyond right now."

"I don't expect you to, Joseph. We both have separate lives we are living and they don't mesh, not even close. We could have a lot of fun for a few days, learn some things about each other, and ourselves, I think." She turned him back around to face her so she could see the expressions that were clear in his eyes. "I want you. I want to feel you inside me. I have a feeling you could teach me a thing or two about sex. I'm willing to be your student. Someday that might come in handy."

He grinned as he shook his head. "You want me to teach you about sex?"

"Yes, actually, I do. I want to know what it's like to be with someone who knows what they are doing and has a handle on how to make sure a woman is taken care of."

"Not a problem, baby. It would be my pleasure to show you how your body can react to certain sensations, touching, stroking, licking, sucking, and everything your body will crave before actual sex occurs."

She brought his hand to her mouth, taking one finger inside to suck like she would his cock if he gave her the chance. Blowjobs were something she enjoyed doing to the guy she was with, not that she had a lot of experience at it, but she liked making a man lose control. When she released his finger, she smiled as she ran her tongue over her lips. "Where can we go?"

"I have my own room in the back part of the barn. It's quiet and private."

"Perfect."

"You're sure?"

"Definitely sure."

He laced their fingers together as he turned and led her down past the stalls to an uncircumspect door off in the corner of the barn. He glanced around him, over his shoulder, and listened before he pulled out a set of keys, unlocked the door, and swept his hand aside to allow her to precede him.

"We won't get into trouble, will we? I mean, you should be working right now."

He held up on finger and pulled out his cell phone. After a moment, he hit a button and put the phone up to his ear. "Hey, Jeff. I'm going to be tied up for a couple of hours. I, uh, had to run into town for a piece of tack that broke while I was cleaning it the other day."

She smiled. A couple of hours would be grand to spend in his arms. They would have to make sure they were very quiet though. Guests would be walking around in the barn and out in the paddocks as well as his brothers.

"Yeah. I'll be back soon." He glanced at his watch. "Hey, can you take out the two o'clock and three o'clock rides? I was scheduled for those, but I will probably have to go to San Antonio to get this piece so I won't be back." He nodded as he smiled over at her. "Yeah, Joshua or Joel can take one and you can take the other, if that works for you."

She began working the buttons on her blouse loose as he continued his conversation with Jeff on the phone. A small giggle escaped her lips as his eyes widened the closer she got to the bottom of the blouse. Her bra was still pushed up around her neck. When she parted the material, her breasts were partially exposed to his darkening gaze. His pupils were now dilated and his face was flush with desire. He swallowed hard when she wet her index finger of her right hand, pushed the material out of the way, and began to run her wet finger around her nipple.

"Uh, yeah. Listen, I need to go so I can get back." He hit end on the phone, tossed it onto the desk next to the wall and stalked closer. "You left the door open."

She glanced behind her. "I did, didn't I."

"Do you want everyone to see what we are about to do?"

She tilted her head to the side, slowly she snaked her hand down her abdomen to where the button at her waist held her pants together, flicked it open, and pushed her hand under the waistband of her jeans and underwear.

"You're a naughty girl."

"Don't you like naughty girls?"

He pushed the door shut, snicked the lock, and turned back to face her. "I love naughty girls." He leaned back against the door, crossing his feet at the ankles, and got comfortable. "Touch yourself."

"I am."

His words came out on a sigh. "Like you mean it. Like you want me to touch you."

She pulled her bottom lip between her teeth as she pushed her jeans and underwear down around her boots. She slid her fingers down to her pussy, wet them with her juices, and then spread it around her clit. The sensation was something she wasn't prepared for as desire rushed through her veins. Her body pulsed with need. Her head felt like it was about to come off her shoulders, all because of the look in his eyes.

The desire radiating off him was something she'd only dreamt about.

He stalked toward her with measured steps, a slow rolling of his hips. "You are so fucking hot right now."

As he got to within a few steps of her, she stopped pleasuring herself and slowly slid her hand up her abdomen to cup her breast and swirl the wet fingertip around her nipple.

With a quick move, she reached around behind herself, unsnapped her bra and pulled it as well as her top off her arms.

He grasped his T-shirt in his hands, tugging it up and over his head, effectively knocking his hat to the floor.

She toed off her boots and dragged her jeans and underwear off her feet before she took a few steps backwards, landing on his bed. Naked as the day she was born, she watched him unbuckled his belt, unfasten his jeans, and push them all to the floor.

When his cock sprang free of the confinement of his jeans, she sucked in a ragged breath before releasing it on a sigh. His cock was long and thick. The head was purple and glistening with a drop of pre-cum on the tip. He definitely wanted her that was for sure.

He dropped in a small chair to toe off his boots and get rid of his jeans.

"You do have a condom, right?"

"Yeah. In the nightstand drawer. I like to be prepared."

She rolled on her side on the bed, pulled open the drawer and had to stifle a giggle as she pulled out a long string of condoms. "Prepared or wishful thinking?"

He grinned as he stood and moved toward her. "I bought them last night after I dropped you off at your car."

"You didn't answer my question."

"A little of both maybe? I knew what I wanted, Rose. I just wanted to make sure you wanted it too."

"From the moment you kissed me at the pond, I wanted this with you."

He frowned as he took the place next to her on the bed. "You are okay with this, right? I mean, you just broke up with your boyfriend. I have no idea how long you'd been seeing him, but I imagine it wasn't just a casual relationship."

"We'd been together for a while, but that doesn't matter now, he doesn't matter now. I don't love him, and I don't want to be with him anymore. Even if you weren't part of the equation, Joseph, this would have been the outcome for him and I. I'd begun to realize that even before I came to Texas and met you." She skimmed her hand over his chest, letting the curls slide through her fingers. "Now are you going to make love to me or not?"

Chapter Eight

Joseph quickly rolled her over onto her back, hovering over her. "You're damned right I'm going to make love to you, fuck your brains out, give you multiple orgasms, and make you feel like you've never felt before."

"Sounds perfect."

He brought their lips together, relishing the softness of hers under his. She felt perfect, more than perfect, she felt amazing. Her lips fit against his so well he was lost to the sensations.

As he skimmed his hand up her side to the under part of her breast, she sucked in a choppy breath. Her eyes were bright and sparkling in the light of his room. Red hair framed her face in small, wispy curls. She apparently didn't spend much time in the sun with her pale complexion. He wasn't surprised though with her features, she probably had some Irish in her and would burn easily.

"You have beautiful breasts. They are the perfect size for my hands." He cupped the right one, feeling the weight of the flesh in his palm. He bent his head and took the nipple into his mouth, biting the tip with small nips.

A moan escaped her lips as her back arched, pushing the flesh into him. "That feels fantastic."

He leaned up, noticing her head was thrown back on the pillow, her eyes were closed, and her mouth was open in a silent sound of ecstasy. The picture was magnificent.

A stroke of his tongue along the underside of her breast brought a groan to the surface. As he continued to brush his tongue over her skin on his way to the red curls at the apex of her thighs, she wiggled under his mouth until he placed his hands at her hips to still her.

"Joseph?"

"Sshh. I'll make you feel good. I promise." He positioned himself between her thighs, kissing the inside of her legs before he nipped at them playfully, and then brought his nose to the crease between her pussy and her thigh. He loved the faint scent of her perfume and the musky smell of an aroused woman.

Her hands were fisted at her sides until he swiped his tongue from her pussy to her clit.

"Oh, God!"

Her thighs opened wider as he continued his planned seduction of her body in order to give her the most satisfaction he possibly could. He wanted to make sure she remembered him and how he made her feel for a long time to come.

Liquid seeped from her pussy as he continued to lick, suck, and eat at her flesh like a starving man. He loved the taste of her and the feel of her under his hands.

She tried lifting her hips to push her clit harder against his mouth, but he held her hips in place with an arm across her pelvis.

He ramped up her pleasure as he slipped two fingers deep into her pussy while still teasing her with his tongue.

Her moans became more frequent and louder until she pulled the pillow from the other side of the bed over her face.

He almost laughed because he knew she was trying to muffle the sounds of her enjoyment from anyone who might be close enough to hear outside their little sanctuary. Personally, he didn't care if anyone heard them.

The moment her orgasm hit, she stuffed the edge of the pillow into her mouth and screamed as she flooded his mouth with her sweetness. He continued to lap at her clit until her orgasm subsided and she pulled the pillow from her face.

"Better?"

"Holy hell, that was fantastic."

He scooted up her body, centering himself over her on his forearms so she didn't have to bear his weight. "I'm glad you liked it."

"I've never, and I mean never ever, had an orgasm like that."

"Didn't your ex ever eat you out?"

"Only when he had to. He sure didn't relish in doing it."

"There is nothing like a woman sedate from an orgasm right before she is built back up again with a cock in her pussy."

"Hmm. You say that like you mean it."

"I do." He grabbed the condom from where it had landed on the bed, sat up, and rolled it down his cock. "Ready for me?"

"Hell yeah."

Surprised at her language and demeanor, he laughed out loud. "I thought you were some shy, quiet little mouse of a girl when I saw you in the diner. Now I realize how outspoken and daring you are." He smiled as he looked down into her eyes. "I can't wait to feel you around me."

"Me either."

He positioned himself at her opening and slowly pushed inside her hot center as he braced himself on his hands. "Holy fuck, you feel good." She'd spread her legs and wrapped them around his hips, bringing her pussy up higher and more in line with his dick. As she shifted her hips in tune with his slow thrusts, he could feel her rubbing her clit along his pelvic bone. His breathing sped up as his heart hammered. Her heartbeat pounding at the base of her neck caught his attention as she threw her head back. Her pussy squeezed his dick in a pulsating rhythm that he knew would send him into a mind-blowing orgasm shortly. "Touch yourself. Rub your clit."

Her hand snaked down between them until he felt it at the top of her mound.

"That's it."

She scooped up some liquid from their joined bodies and began to rub her clit in a fast, circular motion meant to bring her to orgasm quickly. He didn't mind since he was right there too.

His balls drew up against his groin. "You there?"

"Oh yeah. Fuck yeah."

"Come for me, Rose."

She shouted her completion so loud everything outside the room went silent. Unable to hold back his own, he groaned as he continued to pump his hips until he'd emptied everything he had into the end of the condom.

"Shit,' she whispered. "I'm sure everyone outside heard that."

"Yeah, probably." He grinned as she smacked him on the chest.

"Everyone will know what we were doing in here."

"I'm sure they do."

"You aren't helping matters, Joseph."

He sobered slightly, but not much as he rolled off her and peeled off the condom. "What? Don't you think shit is going to hit the fan when Jeff finds out I lied, that I'm really in my room having sex?"

She got to her feet and looked around.

"The bathroom is behind that door over there."

"Thanks." She went through the doorway and closed the door behind her.

He tied the end of the condom and tossed it into the trashcan by the side of the bed, before he laid back, put his hand behind his head, and stared at the ceiling. Sex with Rose had been phenomenal. He couldn't have asked for better. She was giving, sensuous, expressive, and didn't hold anything back. They'd been fantastic together, and he couldn't wait to do it again.

When she opened the door, he had a clear, unobstructed view of her gorgeous body. Red hair framed her face hanging down in long waves around her shoulders, her eyes sparkled, her body was flushed a pretty shade of pink, and her lips were swollen and red from his kisses. She was the most beautiful woman he'd ever seen.

"What?"

"Nothing. Why?"

"You are staring," she said, coming back to the side of the bed and grabbing her clothes from the floor.

"I'm admiring the view. You are a very beautiful woman."

"Thank you, kind sir." She slipped on her underwear and then her bra. "We should probably go out and see what the damage is. Besides, I do need to get some samples this afternoon."

"Yeah, I suppose so. Plus, I'll have to face my brothers when they realize I didn't go to town. Jeff isn't going to be happy I lied to him."

She flipped her hair back over her shoulder after she'd put her shirt in place. "Oh come on. I'm sure he's had sex in the barn before. What about when he was dating his wife?"

"I'm sure they did, although I wasn't keeping track of where and when they spent time together. Some of my brothers still make use of the barn."

She laughed as she pulled on her pants. "That's fantastic. Cowboys having sex in the barn. Classic." When she slipped the button on her jeans through the hole, he finally sat up and threw his legs over the edge over the bed.

Her hair spread down around her shoulders as she finger-combed the tresses into some semblance of order. He took a moment to admire her body. Even in clothes, she was gorgeous and round in all the rights places.

"All right, mister. Up and at 'em. We've got things to do."

"We could fuck again."

A sexy, spirited grin spread across her lips as she placed her hands on her hips. "Later. Right now, you probably have guests you are supposed to be taking care of, a horse to break, or stalls to clean, and I have samples to obtain."

He climbed to his feet and pulled on his jeans, buttoning them at the waist. After he grabbed a clean T-shirt from the drawer, he tugged it over his head, smoothing it down with his hands. "True. Do you need me to take you out to the pond so you can get samples?"

"Are there other water sources on the ranch, other streams or ponds?"

"There are a couple of other streams, yes, but they originate on other properties around us."

"I need to see those as well."

He grabbed his boots from the floor and tugged them on over the socks he'd managed to retrieve. "All right. Let me get one of the others to do the guests rides and we'll take a couple of horses out."

"Uh, Joseph?"

"Yeah?"

"I told you, I've never been on a horse before."

"Oh, right. Okay." He tapped his finger on his chin. How were they going to do this? There were a few places on the ranch that the only way you could get to them was on horseback. "Can you wait to get your samples?"

"I suppose. Why?"

"I need to give you some riding lessons. Some of the spots where we'll need to go aren't reachable by truck. Of course, we could take the four-wheelers. Have you ever been on one of those?"

"No."

He smiled and laughed. "Wow. You really have been sheltered."

The frown on her face told him he'd probably stepped over the line a bit with that remark.

"I am not sheltered. Just because I haven't ridden a horse or been on a four-wheeler doesn't mean I haven't lived, Joseph. Have you walked in Central Park?"

"No."

"Have you been to the theatre and seen a Broadway play?"

"No."

"Have you been to the beaches on Long Island?"

"No."

"Then don't call me sheltered. Our lives have taken different paths, we've experienced different things, but that doesn't mean we shouldn't be open to new things, learn from each other, and see what life has to offer through each other's eyes."

She whipped open the door and stomped out, her irritation clear in her steps as she headed toward the paddock.

He pulled the door shut behind him as he followed, shaking his head as he tried to understand why she was upset. He didn't mean anything by it. New York was like a foreign country to him, so trying to figure out how her life differed from his seemed to something he would have to work on. He liked Rose and wanted to spend more time with her, but he'd never had to deal with someone who seemed to be very opinionated, well, other than his brothers that is.

"Wait up, Rose."

When she turned back around to face him as they approached the doors that lead outside, her hands were on her hips, her face was flushed, and her hair swirled wildly around her shoulders. She was magnificent.

"Let me take you out there. There are a few of the horses that can be cantankerous to be around if they want to be."

"All right." She lowered her gaze to the ground at their feet. "I'm sorry. I didn't mean to get so defensive back there."

He put his finger under her chin and raised her face so he could see her eyes. 'Honey, it's okay. I realize we've grown up very differently and things that are easy and familiar for you, aren't for me and vice versa. If you are willing to learn from me, I'm willing to learn from you." He leaned in, brushing her lips with his. "By the way, you are gorgeous when you're riled up."

"Thank you. I think."

He kissed her again before he turned her around by the shoulders, took her hand and led her outside into the sunshine.

"Where the hell have you been?" Jason scowled as he cinched one of the saddles tighter. "You should have been here to take the last ride out."

"Sorry. I was busy, besides Jeff said he would get someone to take them out for me."

Jason's gaze moved over Rose's face, hair, and clothing before he glowered and turned his back to work on the next animal. "Apparently."

"What?"

"Nothing." Jason glanced his way. "Get ready. The next group will be here shortly to go out."

"Can't you take them?"

"No. I have some other work to do."

"What about Joel and Joshua?" he asked, stopping at the rear of the horse Jason was working with. "Jeff said they would take my two o'clock and three o'clock rides."

"That's when he thought you were going into town, not fucking around in the barn." Jason turned to face him. "We each have a role to play in the running of this ranch, Joey. Yours is wrangler, which means you are in charge of the horses, guest rides, the barn, and the tack. You can't just take off and not be here when it's your turn to do the rides."

"I told you, I was busy."

"Yeah, I could tell."

Joseph glanced at Rose, noting how flushed her face was from embarrassment. "Back off, Jason. I'm allowed free time too."

"Not during the work day."

"Don't fucking tell me what to do. I know there are plenty of times you fucked off during a work day with Peyton when you were supposed to be working."

"Watch your mouth, brother. She's my wife."

"I don't care. Putting a fucking ring on her finger doesn't make it okay for you to do whatever you want during work hours. Every single one of you has taken time off work to have a little playtime with your significant other. I'm doing nothing different than you."

Jason stepped closer, getting close enough Joey could feel Jason's hot breath on his face. "Fucking around with your latest squeeze in the barn is different than us taking personal time with our wives. You don't have anything permanent going on with this girl. She's your latest lay and that's it"

"Take it back, you asshole. Rose isn't like that."

"I won't. Don't tell me you weren't fucking her in your room just a little bit ago. Everyone heard it."

"I said take it back or I will make you wish you hadn't said anything. Rose is a nice girl."

Jason glanced over his shoulder, raking Rose with his gaze. "What the fuck ever."

Joey took two steps back and turned away from his brother. The look in Rose's eyes tore him up. Tears sparkled on her lashes as she pressed her fingers to her mouth. He couldn't stand the embarrassment and mortification on her face.

He spun back around, took the two steps back to Jason's side, and punched him in the mouth.

Jason flew backwards, landing several feet away, blood on his lip and rage on his face. "You didn't fucking just hit me, you asshole."

"Yes, I did. I never once talked about Peyton in any disrespectful manner while you were dating her. I would appreciate the same in return, otherwise we'll be having another talk like this one." He spun around and moved to Rose's side. "I'm sorry." He took her hand, kissed her fingers, and laced the digits together. "Let's go."

"Where are we going?"

"I don't know. I need to stop at the house for a minute, and then we can go wherever you want to go. I need to get the hell away from here before I kill someone."

Hurried steps took them across the yard toward the main lodge. The door swung open under his hand easily as he headed inside, Rose on his heels. When he got the door of the office, he saw his mother sitting at the desk. "Mom?"

Nina looked up, a smile on her face until she caught the look in his eyes and the posture of his body. "What's wrong, honey?"

"I'm taking the rest of the day off."

"What happened?"

"I punched Jason and left him with a bloody lip. Luckily, he wasn't stupid enough to get up before I left the paddock. He said some really nasty things about Rose, and I'm not going to listen to it anymore this afternoon. Rose and I are going into San Antonio or somewhere so I don't kill him."

Nina walked over to him, reaching for the fists clenched at his sides. "It's fine. I'll take care of Jason. You two go on and have a nice afternoon."

"Thanks, Mom."

"Sure, baby. I know how you boys get. I've been dealing with this for years." She smiled as she touched his cheek. "Go out and have some fun. We'll see you in the morning."

He kissed his mom on the cheek before he turned toward Rose, took her hand again, and led her back out into the common room. He didn't want to face any of his brothers right now, afraid of what he'd do if someone else said something derogatory toward Rose. The protective feelings surging through him were odd, but he wasn't about to question them right now. "Where do you want to go?"

Rose stopped him with a hand on his arm. "Joseph, it's okay, really."

"No it's not, Rose. He had no business saying those things, none of them do. They've all been caught at one time or another, playing hooky, fucking in the barn, and doing stupid shit. I'm not saying I'm a saint, far from it, but this is really twofaced of them, all of them. I'm tired of being the baby of the family and getting shit on."

Rose wrapped her arms around his neck, pulling him into a hug. He wasn't sure how to take it. Should he hug her too? Should be pat her on the back to pacify her? Unable to decide, he leaned in and took solace in her comfort.

"It'll be okay. I'm over it. I don't care what they think of me. All I care about is you."

She felt right in his arms, too right. She fit perfectly against his frame. Her arms around him gave him the comfort to walk away from the rage rushing through him. She shouldn't have to be the buffer between him and his brothers, especially when she was the reason for the fight. "I'm sorry."

"Why?" She pulled back in his embrace and he could clearly see the forgiveness in her eyes. "You have nothing to be sorry for."

"For my asshole brother."

"It's a man thing, Joseph. Don't worry about it. All men think a woman who freely gives her body to another without the benefit of a ring, is loose or out for something."

"What the hell, Rose? Not all men think like that."

"Really? Don't you think that way?"

"Not about you."

"Not about me." She smiled, but he could tell she was humoring him into thinking he was smart about the whole thing. "Okay, what about the girl on the phone yesterday? Jessie?"

"What about her?" he asked, afraid he knew where this was going, and he didn't like it.

"Weren't you using her to have sex?"

"I've never slept with her."

"But you would have, given the chance, right?"

Well, fuck.

Chapter Nine

"Well?"

"All right, yeah, I'd planned to have sex with her."

"And?"

"No, I didn't plan to give her a ring or even really date her. I was in it for the sex. Satisfied?" He moved away from her to stare out over the pasture land of the rolling hills through the big front windows. This whole conversation made him feel like an asshole for the way he'd treated women in the past. Yes, he'd used them to get laid without the benefit of a relationship usually. Did that make him a jerk? Yeah, probably.

Rose touched his shoulder. "I wasn't trying to make you feel bad. I wanted you to see that most men thought of women that way until they were ready for something more. There is a double standard in life. Women can't act that way without being called names like whore or slut, but a man doing the same thing is slapped on the back and made to feel proud."

"I understand."

"Do you?"

"Yes." He turned to face her before he placed his hands on her cheeks. "I can't apologize for men all over the world, but I promise, from now on I will not treat women like they are nothing more than a warm place for me to put my dick."

She giggled as she reached up and kissed him on the lips. "Such a poet."

"You still willing to be seen with me while you're here after all of that?"

"Of course! I'm in it for the sex, Joseph, nothing more. I'll be going home in a couple of weeks or whatever, back to my life in New York, and moving on with whatever life is going to throw my way. I don't need the complications of a relationship with you or anyone."

He wasn't sure he liked being used like a… What were they called? Oh yeah, a gigolo. It all seemed rather uncaring. He frowned as she turned back toward the middle of the room and walked toward the pool table. As she began rolling the balls from one end to the other, he realized she really had a different outlook on this whole situation. Most women were all about the ring and the relationship. Here was Rose giving him an out. Sex was it for her and she apparently wanted to experience it with him. *Well, I'll give her the best damned sex she's ever had!*

A second later, he crept up behind her, pulled her back against his chest, and kissed her neck. A shiver rolled through her, one he could feel as his hands moved down her body. Goose bumps rose on her arms. He liked that the touch of his lips did that for her. It made him feel attractive, sexy, and downright invincible. "Let's go somewhere."

"Where?"

"I don't know. How about we get into my truck and just drive, see where it takes us. I have the next couple of days off here at the ranch. We can go to Houston, Austin, or somewhere else. I can show you what the differences are in the area. We can go out to the gulf and hang out on the beach, go swimming in the warm waters, get drunk, be stupid, or do whatever we want. What do you say?"

She turned to face him and wrapped her arms around his neck. "You are a persuasive man, cowboy."

"Is that a yes?"

"Yes." She kissed him on the lips and then leaned back. "But, I have to get some samples first before we leave the area. It does no good for me to have them from Houston."

"All right. I can take you up the road so you can get some from the neighboring property as well as ours."

"I need some from your faucets too. You are on well water, right?"

"Yeah."

"Then if we get some water samples from your faucets, your pond, and maybe one other water source, that should be sufficient for your property. If we can get a few from some of your neighbors, we can call it good for the water. I would need some soil samples too, but I can get those later this week."

"How many samples do you need?"

"As many as I can get, really. The more I have, the easier it is to get a good report microbiologically for the area."

"Why are you doing these tests anyway?"

"The company I work for is thinking of doing some developing out here."

"Like buying up property?"

She shrugged as she wiped her lipstick from his mouth. "I'm not sure what they are doing actually. I don't get into that part of the corporation. They usually check water for contamination because someone has been reported sick or something like that."

He didn't like the idea of a corporation buying up the property out here to develop it. The family had gone through this kind of situation when Terri first showed up. She'd been in the area to check things out for a development firm who had already bought property and planned to put up a housing project. Luckily, Terri had found the nest of an endangered bird on their property. The bird's habitat made it impossible for them to build houses on it.

"What's wrong?"

He shook his head, filing away this information for later. He needed to alert the family if there was going to be an issue again with developers. "Nothing."

"You're frowning."

He took her hand and headed for the door. "It's nothing, really. Let's get these samples you need so we can pack up and head out of town for a couple of days." When he stopped to open the door, he turned toward her. "You're okay with leaving for a couple of days, right?"

"It should be fine. I'm here for a few weeks, so taking a couple of days off to play around won't be a problem."

"Good."

As they walked through the door and out onto the long concrete porch that ran around the entire front of the house, they were greeted by Jeff.

"Where are you going?"

"Out with Rose."

"Don't you have a mare to break this afternoon?"

"Yeah, but it can wait."

Jeff frowned as he glanced to Joey's left where Rose stood, holding his hand. "We don't blow off work, Joey."

"I've already talked to Mom." He stepped closer to Jeff. He stood as tall as his eldest brother and was bulkier because of the work he did. If Jeff wanted to push the issue, he'd push right back. "I'm taking the afternoon off to help Rose get the water and dirt samples she needs for her work. Then we are leaving for a couple of days."

"What the hell?"

"Get over it, Jeff. I rarely take a day off for myself and, by God, I'm doing it right now. All of you have done it a time or two. Now it's my turn." He tugged Rose along behind him as he swept past his brother, leaving him standing on the porch. *They'll be fine. The mare can wait until I come back.* Rose followed him as they went around the house, heading for the barn. "We'll need to go on horseback if we are going to reach the places you need."

"I, uh." She started to drag her feet. "Remember, I've never been on a horse before."

As they breached the doorway of the barn, enveloping them in the scents of horse, hay, and manure, he stopped and turned toward her. "It'll be okay. I'll give you a quick lesson. You'll be fine. The horses here are well-trained. I've trained every one of them, so I know them like the back of my hand."

"Are you sure?"

With both hands framing her face, he said, "Don't worry. I would never let you get hurt on one of our animals." He couldn't help himself, he had to kiss her. When his lips touched hers, he lost himself in the feel of her mouth.

A soft moan escaped her lips, only to be caught in his, as she opened her mouth and allowed him to push his tongue inside. He loved the taste of her, the feel of her, and the way she responded to him. It was like they were meant to find each other in this moment, to experience this together, even if it was only for a short time.

His heart hammered in his chest as he lifted his head and looked down into her eyes. He noticed her pulse beating wildly at the base of her neck as he traced the spot with his finger. "You are so beautiful," he whispered. He pulled her into a hug so he could bury his nose in her hair. The scent he found was intoxicating to his senses. "We need to go, otherwise I'll grab you up and take you back to my place."

"Mmm. I could go for that."

When he stepped back, he had to stifle a groan. His cock was painfully hard. "If we do, we'll never get anything done." He pressed her palm against his erection. "Of course, it's going to be a bitch riding like this."

"Oh, poor baby." Her eyes glittered in the sunlight streaming through the rafters above their heads. "I could take care of that for you. If you want, that is." She licked her lips before bringing the bottom one between her teeth.

"Shit." He dropped his head back. "I would love for you to, but really, we need to get away from here before another one of my brothers decides to give me shit for taking the afternoon off."

"They really do treat you like the baby of the family, don't they?"

"Yeah. It sucks."

She pressed her palm to his cheek. "It'll be okay. I promise." She tilted her head to the side. "We can take a break while we are out riding too. Bring a blanket and a condom."

He liked the way she thought. "You got it, babe."

When he returned a few minutes later, he found her out in the paddock. "I like this one."

He stood behind her, watching as her hands moved over the mare. "You can ride her. She's very gentle. A good mount for a first timer."

She twisted her head around, wrinkling her nose as she glanced back at him. "I'm not sure I like that metaphor."

He laughed at her expression. "There's a first time for everything." He moved in so he covered her back from shoulders to buttocks. "Ever had anal sex?"

"Mmm. No."

"First time for everything."

She sighed as she rubbed her buttocks against his hard-on. "Maybe."

He buried his nose in the crook of her neck. The natural scent of her skin drove him crazy. "You are hell on my body, lady."

"Good. I like the thought of keeping in you on your toes, cowboy."

She shivered under his touch when he rubbed his whiskered jaw along her neck, abrading the skin to a slight redness. The paleness of her skin showed the abrasion like a brand. He liked the thought of that a little too much.

After he cleared his throat and stepped back, she turned toward him with a little smile curling the corners of her mouth.

"Will you help me up?"

"Sure." He helped her turn, slide her foot into the stirrup, and then boosted her up with a helpful hand to her ass. When she glanced down and gave him a reprimanding look, he grinned and shrugged. "Let's go through some basics of riding now that you are comfortably in the saddle." As he went through how to guide the horse left and right, he couldn't help but admire her seat in the saddle, her ease with the reins, and how well she took instruction. "Now pull back on them to stop her."

A beautiful smile spread across her lips. "I think I got it."

"If you want her to trot, you can press her sides with your knees." He watched her guide the mare around the paddock in a slow trot. She was doing a great job for someone who'd never been on a horse before. When she brought the animal to a stop near him, he gave her an approving nod. "You did fantastic."

"Thank you. Coming from an expert, that means a lot."

"I'm no expert by any means."

"Sure you are. You've trained all these animals to be different levels for different rider abilities. That's a big feat."

He could feel the heat rushing up to his face. Compliments weren't something he was used to, not from strangers anyway. He frowned. She really was a stranger to him if he thought about it. He'd only known her a few days, but it sure seemed like he'd known her a lot longer.

Clearing his throat, he adjusted the hat on his head and moved to where his own mount stood tied to the pole. "Are you ready to go?"

"Uh, one thing. I need my bag from the car. It has my sample kit in it for the water and soil samples I need."

"If you give me your keys, I'll go fetch it for you."

"Sure." She pulled the keys from the front pocket of her jeans, dangling them in front of him as he reached up to grab them. "There is a small duffle type bag in the backseat."

When he returned a few minutes later, he saw Jeremiah talking with her as he stood near the mare's nose.

"Jeremiah."

"Hey, Joey." Jeremiah continued to stroke the horse's nose. "I was talking with your friend, and she said you two were going out riding. I thought you had a mare to break this afternoon."

"I do, but I'm taking the afternoon off."

"Oh?"

"Yeah. Rose needs a guide so she can get the water and dirt samples she needs for her work."

"That's right. I'm here in Bandera to gather samples for the company I work for in New York."

"I see." Jeremiah's eyes narrowed.

Joey knew thoughts were running through his brother's head, the same as his. After running into a similar situation when Terri showed up in Bandera a few years ago, they were all wary of people snooping around the property too much, wanting information. He'd have to do a little more digging on the company she worked for.

"Here you go." He helped secure the small bag to the back of her saddle before moving toward where his gelding stood tied. Once he was mounted, he headed toward the back of the paddock that led out onto the many trails running through Thunder Ridge.

Sunshine beat down on their heads, making sweat trickle down his back between his shoulder blades. He removed his hat, wiping wetness from his forehead and letting the slight breeze ruffle his hair before he put it back on. He turned in his saddle, glancing back at Rose. "You okay?"

"Yes, but I'm going to be really sore, I think."

"Yeah, you will, but I have some great ointment to help with those sore muscles." He grinned as she shifted in the saddle. "I love having my hands all over you."

"I like that too, cowboy."

"We should be there shortly. It's just over the ridge."

"Good. My ass is killing me."

He chuckled as they crested the hill where the small pond sat. An underground stream fed this particular spot and the run trickled down to an area outside the horse's pen at the back of the house. It was a constant source of water for them, even in the heat of the summer.

When he stopped his gelding and dismounted, he ground tied the animal before moving to her side. "Here. Let me help you down."

He reached up his hands as she brought her leg over the pommel, and then slid down into his arms. As her toes hit the ground, he looked down into her bright green eyes. He stood there just drinking her in.

He lowered his head until their lips were a hairsbreadth apart. His breath mingled with hers. Her eyes dilated so the pupils were big and black, almost covering the irises of her eyes. Kissing her seemed like the best thing to do at the moment, and Lord did he love kissing her. Grazing her lips with his, he barely brushed them across hers so it wasn't really a kiss, but a tease of things to come. Her heartbeat hammered at the base of her neck, matching his own erratic rhythm.

He cupped her cheek. The softness of her skin beneath his touch made his palm tingle. He slid his fingers down so he could wrap his hand around her neck, caressing the bounding pulse at the base with his thumb.

Wrapping her braid around his other hand, he pulled her head back, baring her neck to his touch. He grazed his teeth across the silky surface, forcing a moan from her mouth. A little nip along her jawline had her grasping his biceps as she shivered under his touch. *So responsive.*

With one leg now wedged between her parted thighs, he pulled her down so she straddled his thigh. His cock rested against her belly, throbbing behind the fly of his jeans. He wanted to be inside her wet, grasping pussy so badly he could hardly stand to take this slow.

Two fingers flicked the button on her jeans loose before he parted the material to reveal her silky panties. He slipped his hand down the back of her pants, grasping her buttocks in his palm. All he could think about was being in her ass. That would come in time, if she was around long enough.

He pushed back slightly so he could look at her. Her skin glowed, it was so pale. Freckles dotted her exposed flesh, now pink from the sun. He would have to loan her his hat for the trip back.

She gasped as he pulled her pelvis closer to him, letting her ride his leg. "I need you to make love to me, Joseph."

"Soon, sweetheart, very soon."

She wrapped her legs around his waist, leaning into the side of the horse for balance. "Fuck me here, right here."

He forced her legs back down so she stood on the ground. "Let me grab the blanket. We'll go down by the creek. There is a small sandy area where we can take our time and get this right."

A sigh escaped her lips and she brought the bottom one in between her teeth.

He moved back toward his horse to retrieve the blanket and the condoms he brought, before returning to her side, taking her hand, and leading her down by the water.

His balls ached with the need to come. He hadn't been this horny in a long time.

They stopped near the stream, and he turned to face her. He brought her hands up to his mouth, kissing her knuckles before he released her and spread the blanket down on the sand. Once he got it all out and straight, he took her hands, drawing her down with him on the soft makeshift bed.

He brought both hands up to cup her face. "I love how your skin glows. It's so soft to touch, I could skim my fingers over you all day long. Your eyes are so expressive, I can tell what you are feeling every time I look into them. Your body is so responsive to mine, it's incredible. It makes me feel invincible seeing the desire in your gaze."

"I want you."

"I want you too. I need you so bad, I hurt."

She reached for his belt buckle, tugging on it until it was loose and hanging at the waistband of his jeans. Her hand cupped his erection, skimming up and down, making him moan low in his throat and his eyes roll back.

"Easy, darlin'. I want to be inside you when I come."

"Don't worry. I know how far to push you before you explode." She brushed her lips over his, tentatively touching her tongue to his mouth.

He opened for her, allowing her tongue in to duel with his as he buried his hands in her hair. He wished it was loose.

He would love to tangle his hands in the strands as he rode her mouth.

As if she heard his thoughts, she urged him to follow her up on her knees while continuing their kiss. After she tore her mouth from his, she worked the buttons out of their holes so his shirt hung off him and she could run her mouth down his chest. She stopped to flick his nipples with her tongue before biting at the tip.

"Fuck."

"Mmm. Yes, we will." Her hands worked at the button on his jeans until she had it open and she could push them down around his thighs.

His cock sprung free, relieving him of a little pressure, but now he strained up and proud, waiting for her mouth.

The moment she encircled the head with her lips, he shivered as he fought to keep from coming so soon. Even though he couldn't wrap his hands in the strands of her hair, he did wind the braid around his fist, guiding her in her task. The heat of her mouth drove his desire to explosive. His thighs ached from holding still.

She fingered the skin between his balls and his ass, sliding them up and down, dragging deep moans from his throat.

He almost came apart when she pressed her finger into his ass. No one had ever done that before. Pulling away, he sat back on his boot heels. "Holy hell, woman. Are you trying to kill me?"

She grinned as she ran her hand around his cock. "You didn't like it?"

"It was awesome, but different. Where did you learn that?"

"Someone in my past used to enjoy it. Not all men do, but I thought I'd see what you thought."

He shakily got to his feet, toed off his boots, and then stripped off his jeans. "Strip." Some time while she was sucking his cock, he'd lost his hat behind him. He didn't care. His cock hurt, he was so hard.

She stood and took her clothes off as quickly as she could. When she stood naked in front of him, he reached out a shaky hand, circling her areola with his fingertip. She leaned into his touch as she dropped her head back. Goose bumps broke out on her skin.

With his fist around his hard flesh, he leaned in and took her nipple between his lips. The nub hardened as he sucked.

She shoved her fingers through his hair, holding his head against her breast. "Oh, yeah." Whimpers escaped her mouth as he sucked and nipped at the flesh. After a few minutes, she sank down on the blanket, drawing him down with her as he kissed her again.

He ran his mouth over her skin from her lips, down her neck, across her breasts, and down her belly until he reached the juncture of her thighs. She spread her legs, giving him the space he needed. The scent of peaches reached his nose. "You smell fantastic."

She giggled. "It's my lotion."

"I don't care. I love the smell." He buried his nose near her mound and inhaled. "It makes me want to eat you all the more."

"Please do. I love having my pussy licked."

He licked her clit once, then twice. She spread her thighs farther apart as her breath came out in panting spurts. Her clit had begun to swell and turn a bright red, just like he wanted. He bit the tip of the bud, driving a deep, throaty moan from her lips.

"God, Joseph, please."

He forced his hands up under her buttocks so he could bring her closer to his mouth. As he continued licking and sucking, the moans he heard thrilled him. She definitely enjoyed this and he couldn't be happier.

When he pushed two fingers into her pussy and licked her clit quickly, she screamed loud and high as her climax rolled over her.

He continued to lick softly against her clit, bringing her down slowly until she sighed and relaxed into the blanket. Brushing a quick kiss to the inside of her right thigh, he reached over to grab his jeans and retrieve the condoms he'd brought.

A giggle escaped her lips when he pulled out the string. "Just how many times are you planning on fucking me while we are out here?"

Embarrassment flushed his cheeks with heat. "Well, I, uh…"

She sat up and put her hand on his face. "It's okay. I'm hoping we can use them all."

"Maybe by the end of the day, but not all at once."

"Are you saying you can't—" She grabbed the strip and counted them out. "Come six times in an hour?"

"Yeah, probably not."

"I'm so disappointed, Joseph." Her grin softened that statement.

"You are in so much trouble, girl."

Her eyes widened in mock fear as she pressed the strip of condoms to her chest. His eyebrow went up as she tore one off with her teeth. When she had it opened, she moved closer, got up on her knees, and rolled it down his cock. She leaned in and brought her mouth close to his. "Is that a promise?"

Damn, she's a sight! He crushed his mouth against hers, taking what he wanted from her willing lips as she caressed his cock with her hand. By the time they were both breathing hard, he let her mouth go so he could get to the fucking. Boy, was he ready for that part. He lay on his back, pulling her with him so she could straddle his hips. She took instruction well as he helped her position herself across his middle. Her hot pussy almost scalded him when he pushed his cock up and just barely inside her. She tossed back her head, braced her hands on his chest, and moaned long and loud.

As she took him inside her body, she rolled her pelvis forward, riding his cock like it was the last time she would ever have sex. He slipped in and out of her, feeling her vagina grip him like a vice. The walls contracted as he felt her quiver around him.

"Fuck, Rose, you are so gorgeous like this. Ride me, honey." He grasped both her breasts in his palms, kneading them with his fingers before he took each nipple between his first finger and his thumb to roll them. The dusky nipples turned a deep rose color as her need skyrocketed.

With her face to the sky, her eyes were closed, her mouth tight with desire, and body flush with need. Lord, she was beautiful as she moved over him.

Her long red hair brushed against his thighs, tickling the skin. The pain in his cock pulled his balls up tight against his groin with the need to come, but he needed to make sure she got her orgasm before he could take pleasure in his.

She continued to rub her clit along his pelvic bone while she rode his cock.

He reached down between them with one hand, took the swollen little nub between his fingers, and pinched it *hard*.

Her orgasm rolled over her in a wave he could see as she cried out her pleasure to the air around them in a long, loud scream.

His own orgasm ripped through him, surging up from his balls before shooting out the end of his cock like a rocket.

When Rose collapsed across his chest, he could feel her rapid breathing against his neck, the sweat clinging to her body as he skimmed his hands down her back, and the softness of her hair against his palm.

She fit against him perfectly.

He wasn't sure where this train of thought was headed, but he sure didn't like it. Nope. Not one bit.

Chapter Ten

The heat from Joseph's gaze rested on her back as she bent down and scooped up some soil from a spot where they'd stopped the horses. She needed several samples of both water and dirt to send back to the company. They'd had a few reports of contaminated water from an anonymous source, but she couldn't see the Young family operating their guest ranch knowing they had contaminated water. They didn't seem to the type of family that took advantage of people like that. She had to be sure though, and the only way to do that was to test for every microorganism they could think of in the lab.

When she stood, she turned to face him, excited by where his gaze rested before coming up to her face. "Joseph?"

"Yeah?"

"I think I have what I need from your ranch, except for getting a few water samples from the house and a couple of the guest cabins."

"All right."

"I do need to see if I can get some from a couple of your neighbors though. Is that a possibility?"

"I'm sure I can talk to some of them."

"A few from some of your direct neighbors would be great."

He frowned.

"Something wrong?"

"No. I guess not."

"You don't sound so convincing."

"Well, one of our neighbors is The Marshalls. They aren't too friendly with us or should I say with me."

"Oh?"

"Yeah. Jessica's Old Man Marshall's daughter."

"*The* Jessica from the phone call?"

"Yep."

"I see." She didn't like the thought of Joseph with another woman. *Easy girl. He's only yours temporarily.* She took a deep breath as she tried to calm the cramp in her stomach. "Maybe if I go there by myself he would be okay with it."

"Maybe. I can show you where to go, but it's probably not a good idea for me to go with you. He'd be more likely to shoot at me than welcome me to his porch."

"Shoot at you? What the hell did you do the last time you were there?"

He dropped his gaze to the tips of his boots, scuffing them in the dirt. "We were both half naked when he found me there the last time. He chased me out to my truck shooting at me with buckshot in his shotgun."

She busted out laughing so hard she snorted and tears rolled down her cheeks. He frowned at her when she took a seat on a large rock because she thought she was about to pee her pants. "Oh my God! That's priceless!" She rolled off the rock onto her hands and knees as she giggled hysterically.

"It really wasn't that funny, Rose. He dented my tailgate something fierce with that shit."

She laughed harder. She could only image him running across this man's lawn holding his jeans up with one hand, his boots in the other, all while trying to avoid getting buckshot in his ass. After she'd calmed down a little, she wiped her face, and looked up at him. "I'm sorry, Joseph, but it's hilarious to think of you running across their lawn in your bare feet, trying to avoid getting shot."

Even though he had a frown on his face, he held out a hand to help her to her feet. "We should be getting back if we are planning to go to Houston tonight. It's a four hour drive."

When she managed to calm her giggles, she replied, "Wow, really?"

"Yeah."

"Are you sure you want to go there? I'm sure we can find stuff to do a little closer."

"It's up to you. You haven't been here before. I want to show you what Texas is all about, so you have some good memories to take home."

Trailing her fingertips down the buttons on his shirt, she glanced up through her lashes and caught him staring at her lips. No matter that they'd had sex less than an hour ago, she still wanted him as need clawed low in her belly. Desire had never had her in its clutches like this with Brandt or anyone else in her past for that matter, and it seemed like it wasn't about to let her go until she'd got this cowboy out of her system. "We could go back to my hotel room."

"That place is a dump. You should take a room at Thunder Ridge. Then you'd be close."

"Close enough for what?"

"I could visit you."

"Would you?"

"Hell yeah. Every chance I got."

Up on her toes, she placed her hands on his shoulders and brushed her lips against his in a very light caress. "I like the sound of that."

"Then let's get you settled in a room."

They mounted their horses and set out back toward the main lodge. She kind of liked the idea of being close to

Joseph, but it also gave her a chance to check things out around the ranch and the places nearby.

As she watched his back while they rode, she loved the way his shirt stretched across the surface. It molded nicely to his broad shoulders, giving her a great view of his muscles. His ass fit into the rear of the saddle spectacularly too. There sure was something about a cowboy in a pair of Wranglers.

When they rode into the yard a little while later, the scene made her smile. His brothers were bustling around, taking care of what needed on the ranch. It fascinated her to watch them working, their hands busy with tasks that she'd never even thought of living in New York.

They dismounted in front of the barn, and Joseph took the horses inside to do whatever it was they do, while she stood outside in the sun, stretching her abused muscles. Her ass hurt from riding, and the inside of her thighs screamed from the mistreatment of having sex on the hard ground and being spread around the girth of the horse. She moaned softly, not fully aware of the audience of women nearby.

Mesa walked over, touching her on the shoulder. "Are you okay?"

She glanced up and smiled. "I'm fine, just sore from the ride."

"Have you been on a horse before?"

"No, never."

Mesa laughed. "You'll be a lot more sore tomorrow, I'm afraid. I had the same affliction after I got here."

"How long have you and Joel been married?"

"About six years now."

"That's awesome. I hope someday to say the same thing."

"He's my world outside of our kids. I can't imagine my life without him, this ranch, and our family."

"I can imagine."

Joseph came out of the barn a minute later, carrying her duffle. "Come on. Let's get you a room. I know there should be one available. Mesa's group of friends is leaving this afternoon."

Mesa smiled. "Yes, they are. I'm glad they came. It's been a great week, but I'm ready for some quiet around here for a few days."

"I bet it gets crazy in the summer."

"Yes, it does. We have a crowd every week, it seems."

Rose waved to Mesa as Joseph took her hand and led her inside. Nina met them in the main room. "Well, hello there."

"Mom, Rose needs a room. One of the cabins would be great."

Nina's eyebrow went up. "Let's see what we can find." She turned around to head into the registration office. "I have one near the back of the compound. It's private and not attached to another room."

"That would be good," Joseph replied before Rose had a chance to answer.

"I think Rose can answer for herself, Joseph."

Rose gave him a sideways glance. "Yes, I can, and yes, that would fine."

Once she gave Nina her business credit card and had her key in hand, Joseph walked her back out toward her car. "I can get my stuff from my hotel room and be back in about an hour."

"Want me to go with you?"

"You don't have to, Joseph. I know you have some things to do around here."

"I took the afternoon off, remember?"

"I know, but it sounds like your family is having a problem with you doing that."

He pulled her close to his chest. "Too bad. This is our time."

She fingered the top button on his shirt. "I know, but I don't need to piss off your family for dragging you away from your work."

"They'll get over it." He brushed his lips over hers in a brief kiss. "If you'd rather go by yourself, that's fine."

"I probably should. I need to call the office anyway to check in."

His brow furrowed for a second. "Sure."

"All right. I'll be back in a couple of hours and then we can decide what to do for the rest of the evening."

He stepped back so she could open the door on her car and held it for her. "Be careful."

"I will."

As she started her car to go back into Bandera and get her things, she wondered what the evening would bring. Making love with Joseph was phenomenal, and she couldn't wait to do it again. Did that make her a slut? She shrugged. *Whatever. I'm going to enjoy this and worry about consequences later.*

She only had a few days left here in Texas before she needed to go home. She planned to make the most of it with one hot cowboy.

About an hour later, she'd packed her things and sat down at the table in her room to call her boss at work. They'd already planned a conference call today, so she figured she might as well do it while she had the chance.

As the phone rang, she contemplated what she'd found out on Thunder Ridge. No one knew what the water and soil held until they examined it under a microscope. Even finding tiny particles of contaminates could shut down the ranch. She hoped that didn't happen. The family there would be devastated should something like that be brought to light.

"Rose?"

"Hello, Mr. Albright."

"Hello. How is Texas?"

She took a sip of the can of Coke in her hand. "Interesting place. I've met some of the locals."

"Don't forget, you are there on business."

"I know. I'm enjoying the area on my off time. I'm getting what you need. Don't worry."

"I hope so. We need that information as soon as possible. The investors, uh, I mean the community needs to know whether there are any problems near there."

She frowned. *Investors? What the hell is he talking about?* "I have the samples from Thunder Ridge. I need to get some from the neighbors next door. I'm going over there tomorrow."

"Good, good. You have the FedEx information to send those samples when you have them."

"Yes."

"I'm looking forward to seeing the results."

Odd. He's never taken an active interest in this stuff before. "Anyway, do you want me to call you when I have the other samples?"

"Yes, please. I assume then you'll be on your way back to New York?"

"Yes, sir."

"I'm looking forward to having you back in the office, Rose."

"Thank you, sir. I will talk to you tomorrow or the next day."

"That's fine. Talk to you then."

"Bye." She hung up the phone, frowning at it for a moment as the conversation played over in her head. The company she worked for was a microbiology lab that tested water and soil samples for a variety of reasons, usually involving complaints filed with the county. Something sounded awfully fishy with this. Digging a little deeper into the situation might be in order.

She grabbed her suitcases and opened her motel room door. The sun was shining, the birds were singing, and there were a few locals about on the streets. Trucks zipped by without a care in the world, some blaring country music, some jacked up so high she would need a stepstool to get inside. The light at the center of town turned to red in the distance. Life went on whether she stood on the threshold of something new or not. Right now she wasn't sure, but her whole world seemed like it was about to be turned upside down, and she didn't know how to stop it.

When she arrived back at the ranch about half an hour later, she was caught by surprise to find Joseph waiting for her near the driveway. It made her happy to see him as he stepped up near the car as she stopped. "Well, hello."

"Hi," he replied as she stepped out. He leaned in and kissed her on the mouth.

"What a way to be greeted. You don't meet all the guests like this, do you?"

"Nope. Only you."

"Such a charmer." She shut the door and moved around to the back of the car to grab her suitcase. Joseph took it out of the trunk before she could reach for it. "I can get it."

"A lady doesn't carry her own bags when there is a cowboy around." He jingled the key to her cabin in front of her eyes. "I come bearing the key."

She smiled as she shut the trunk and followed him to her cabin. When he opened the door for her, she got her first look at the interior. A huge king sized bed with a wrought iron headboard and footboard took up most of the room. The coverlet on the bed specifically drew her attention to the beautiful wedding ring pattern in multiple colors. "Wow. This place is gorgeous."

"I'm glad you like it. It's one of my favorite cabins. We use it as a honeymoon suite." He pushed open the door to the right. "The bathroom is in here. It's got a huge soaking tub with jets."

"Oh my. My body will love that a little later. The ride earlier took its toll on my thighs."

He moved to her side, coming up behind her as she turned toward the window to look outside. The hills in the distance captured the dying evening light in shadows of black, purple, and blue.

Joseph put his hands on her shoulders before running his hands up and down her arms. "I promised to help with the soreness in those muscles. After supper I'll give you a good rub down with some special stuff."

"I can't wait," she whispered, tipping her head back on his shoulder.

The bell clanged in the distance signaling supper was ready.

He brushed his lips over her neck, giving her a little nip before he moved away. "Let's go get some food so we can get this party started."

A shivered rolled down her back as the heat from his chest left her cold when he stepped back. "All right."

Supper was an interesting affair. Most of Mesa's group had left, so the main lodge seemed quiet in comparison. The family still took up a big portion of the room at the end, but the guests had thinned out a lot, leaving empty tables.

She listened as conversation went around the table. Jeff brought up things on the ranch requiring attention tomorrow. Nina talked about the bookings for the coming week. Jonathan mentioned some new website stuff he was working on. Jeremiah talked about a new upstart company he wanted to invest some of the family's money in. Rose frowned when he mentioned the name of the company. Something was familiar about it, but she couldn't place it just yet.

"What kind of company is it, Jeremiah?" James asked, before taking a bite of his food.

"It's a development company that I've been talking to about our land."

"What the hell are you talking about?" Jeff asked, his voice hard and sharp.

"Don't get all bent out of shape, Jeff. This would be a good thing for Thunder Ridge."

"How do you figure? If someone wants to come in and take over the area for whatever purpose that can't be good for ranches like ours. We went through that when Terri got here and the development company who bought up the neighbor's ranch wanted to put houses in."

"This company isn't wanting to put in houses. They're here to test for oil."

"Oil?" Nina laid her fork on the table. "As in oil wells?"

"Yes, Mom."

"I don't like the sound of this, Jeremiah. It sounds risky."

"All investments are risky, but if we get in on the ground floor, this could be great for us."

"We don't need the money, son," his father added. "You've already seen to that."

"I understand, Dad, but think about it. If we hit oil on our property, none of us would ever have to work again."

Rose wanted to say something. Being a microbiologist, she knew the signs of possible oil on a property and the changes it would make in the surrounding landscape. Thunder Ridge as a guest ranch would cease to exist once the oil drillers came in. They would level everything to put up the wells. They would tear up the countryside. The cattle wouldn't be able to graze here anymore because of the contamination to the water. She started to shake.

"What's the name of the company, Jeremiah?" James folded his hands on the tabletop as the conversation went on around them.

"Mission Drilling."

Joseph turned toward her, taking her hand in his warm one. "Rose?"

"I, uh, I need to leave, Joseph, please?"

"What's wrong?"

She knew that name. She'd seen it several times on documents at the office where she worked. They were in the market to shut out the small ranchers, farmers, and land owners. They used her company to prove the water was contaminated and the owners of the property couldn't continue to run a business or live on their property, making their land worthless and unusable. The drilling company would buy the land cheap, knowing there were probably deep pockets of rich oil, and then drill, making millions. "Please. Let's just go."

"All right."

Joseph brought her to her feet, bringing all eyes on them. "Rose isn't feeling well. I'm going to take her back to her cabin."

"Are you all right, Rose?" Nina asked climbing to her feet and moving toward them.

"Yes. I'll be fine. I guess I overdid today with the ride and the sun."

"Do you need anything, honey? I can have the cook make you some soup or something."

"No. I'll be fine, Mrs. Young."

"Nina, honey, call me Nina."

"Nina. Thank you. I think I'll go onto bed and rest. I'll be fine tomorrow."

"Good night then. Rest well."

Joseph led her down the center of the main lodge dining room, out the side door to walk her toward her cabin in the distance. Darkness had fallen, but the path was lit by individual lights along the walkway.

They'd left the light on inside the room when they'd left earlier. Now, it was a beacon in the night to her soul. She needed to think.

"Rose?" His voice held a question, one she wasn't sure she could answer.

"I'm okay, Joseph. I need to relax, take a bath, and get some sleep, I think." She touched his cheek as he held her in his arms. She liked how he wanted to take care of her. Leave it to the cowboy to want to help. "I'll be fine in the morning." The disappointment in his eyes hurt her heart. "I'm sorry. I wanted us to be able to spend tonight together."

"It's okay, darlin'. If you aren't feeling well, then I'll take a raincheck."

"Thank you."

He kissed her on the nose and stepped back. "Sleep well, sweetheart."

When he disappeared into the night, she sighed. It was so hard when a person really liked someone but knew it could go nowhere. A few days of happiness, good sex with an amazing man, and the welcoming feeling of family here on the ranch couldn't replace the depression she felt surrounding her heart.

I have a really bad feeling about this.

Chapter Eleven

Rose spent the next morning on the Internet and pooling her resources to find out as much as she could about Mission Drilling. The information wasn't what she wanted to hear. She had a few contacts on the inside of the company since her boss had done business with them before, and she'd been their lead biologist on different projects.

When Joseph had come by the cabin, she'd feigned still not feeling well.

"Is there something I can get you, Rose?"

"No, Joseph. I'm okay. Rest is the best thing for me. Besides, I'm sure you have work to do today since you took yesterday off to take me around."

"Yeah, I do. I really need to work with the mare I need to break, plus we have a load of feed coming in this morning and riders to take out." He touched her cheek and frowned. "You do feel a little warm. Maybe you are coming down with something."

"Maybe. I'll take a couple of Tylenol and sleep for a few hours. I'll see you in the barn later or at lunch. Okay?"

"All right. Rest up and we'll talk later."

She watched as he stepped off her small porch and headed toward the barn. Deceiving him didn't sit well with her, but she had to find out what the hell this Mission Drilling wanted with Thunder Ridge land. She couldn't go riding by herself to check out the area since she didn't do well on horseback, and her car wasn't up to driving over some of the dirt roads around here either. Information is what she needed. Tapping her fingers to her lips as she sat back in the chair in front of her computer, she contemplated how to proceed.

The samples still had to be obtained from the neighbors and Joseph mentioned the Marshalls. If she could get samples from their property, she might be able to prove drilling here wouldn't be a good idea. Then again, if she sent those samples into her boss, they would have the information they needed to declare the area contaminated, thus forcing the locals to move out.

If she could find a local biology lab to run the tests without alerting the company she worked for and got the results she needed, she could forestall the issue.

She would likely lose her job over this if they found out, and possibly her livelihood. A microbiologist with the reputation for bucking against her employer wouldn't be employable anywhere else. Doing the right thing meant more than her job though.

If the family finds out I know more about this than I'm letting on, they won't be happy, I'm sure.

"If I can save their land, it will be worth it."

For the next couple of hours, she found out all she could about oil drilling, water contamination, soil issues, and Mission Drilling.

The company had been around for a number of years, twelve to be exact, and had made millions drilling for oil in Texas on land they'd bought that wasn't inhabitable because of one reason or another. They were owned by two brothers.

When she typed their names into the Internet search, she found an interesting tidbit. Their third cousin by marriage was Walter Albright. "Son of a bitch. My boss is their cousin? Holy hell. No wonder he wants these samples like yesterday. Even if there is no contamination and everything checks out, God knows how he might tamper with them to say this land is unusable. It doesn't matter whether they have been ranching this area for a couple hundred years or not."

She heard a tap on the door and looked at the clock. It was almost noon.

"Rose?"

Joseph. "Just a second." She closed her laptop, shuffled the papers she'd been jotting on into the desk, and straightened her clothes. Her hair was a disaster. She looked down to realize she hadn't even gotten dressed yet. *Oh well, it lends itself to the story of me being ill.* She really hated lying to Joseph, but if it meant helping his family, she'd do whatever it took.

When she opened the door, she was struck by the man again. He really was the epitome of the cowboy with his hat pulled down to shade his eyes from the sun, the western button-down shirt stretched across his chest, the formfitting jeans, and the dusty boots. Her mouth watered to run her tongue over every inch of his skin and listen to him moan.

"You look like hell."

"Thanks, Joseph."

"Do you feel any better?"

"Yeah. I'm okay. I just need to shower."

His lips lifted in a little grin. "I could join you. I'm pretty dirty from working with that mare all mornin'." His gaze traveled down her frame, making her nipples pebble into hard little nubs. "Of course, I don't have any clean clothes with me."

"Did she give you trouble?"

"Some, yeah. She didn't like having me on her back."

"Are you okay?"

"I'm good. Nothing new for me." He stepped across the threshold of her cabin when she moved back to let him inside. "I could go grab some clothes and be back in a second to join you."

"Sounds good to me."

He touched her cheek. "Are you sure you are feeling up to it?"

"I'm fine, Joseph, and I really want you to make love to me." She brushed her mouth against his, taking in the taste of his lips. He was everything she wanted right now.

"I'll be right back then."

When he disappeared out the door in a flash, she couldn't help but smile. She planned to give as good as she got until this whole thing was over, either way.

After she stepped into the bathroom to warm up the shower, she hummed a tune to herself while she stripped off her pajamas and underwear.

A moment later, she heard the door open and then close. *Wow. That didn't take long.* When he didn't appear in the bathroom, she opened the door and peered out. No one was in the room. *Now, that's weird.*

She shivered in the cool air from the bedroom before she shut the door, letting the steam from the shower soothe her. She'd heard there were ghosts on the place and apparently one was paying her a visit.

Joseph returned a few minutes later. "Rose?"

"In the bathroom waiting for you."

When he came through the door, he wasn't wearing a stitch of clothing. The smattering of chest hair tempted her to touch with her fingertips, but his cock was what she really wanted. With her fingers wrapped around his length, she guided him toward her mouth as she knelt on the bath rug.

He wrapped his hands in her hair, fisting her scalp to the point of stinging. She loved feeling him take what he wanted as he fucked her mouth.

A groan rumbled from between his lips. "Holy crap, Rose."

She hummed her satisfaction against his flesh. Having him in her mouth drove her need to explosive. She wouldn't be able to hold back very long when he finally pushed inside her.

After bringing him to the brink of losing all control, she stood, took his hand, and led him into the tiled shower stall.

Soap suds slid down his chest as she smoothed her slick hands over his chest, down his abdomen, and around his cock. She loved the feel of his skin beneath her hands, every plane, and every muscle.

He backed her under the spray to wet her hair before he grabbed the shampoo and scrubbed her scalp. No one had ever washed her hair in the past and to have his hands there felt amazing.

Once her hair was squeaky clean, he soaped her body up, paying close attention to all the hidden spots that had her panting. Around her breasts he moved, weighing each one in his palm before he rinsed it clean and then sucked on the nipple until she squirmed. "God, Joseph. You're driving me crazy."

"I like to give as good as I get."

He pushed her down on the little bench seat in the corner of the stall, dropped to his knees, and then started to lick her pussy like a dying man enjoying his last sip of water. Her body broke out in goose bumps. She rested her legs over his shoulders, loving what he was doing to her body.

Moments later, he slid two fingers into her pussy as he continued to lick and suck at her clit.

Her orgasm crashed over her without much warning, bursting into stars behind her eyelids as she cried out her pleasure with his name on her lips.

Once she came down from her high, he picked her up, wrapped her legs around his waist, and then slid into her in one thrust. The feeling wasn't anything she could remember ever having before.

"Fuck."

"What?"

"I don't have a condom."

"It's fine. I'm clean and on the pill."

His gaze fixed on hers, looking deep into her soul. She could see the debate in his eyes. Did he want to take the chance and go ahead with this or pull out and walk away?

"Joseph?"

"Ah hell." He moved a little before thrusting again. "I can't stop."

"Thank God."

He chuckled before he groaned deep in his throat and pressed his forehead against her. "You feel fantastic, Rose. Going bare with you is amazing. You are so tight, so good."

She couldn't say a word as he continued slowly thrusting his hips, driving his cock deep into her pussy time and time again. Every inch of him touched her, making her want to take him inside her and keep him there forever.

Shit. This is bad.

* * * *

Joseph watched Rose as she talked to his mother at lunch. Something was different, but he couldn't put a finger on what.

Sex in the shower had been fantastic. He couldn't remember when he'd experienced something like that before. He knew he hadn't.

The feeling she was hiding something from him had him on edge though, and he couldn't shake it.

"Rose, didn't you say you were a microbiologist?" Jeremiah asked from his spot two seats down.

"Yes. I'm here taking samples of the water and soil."

"Why?"

She bit the inside of her lip as she glanced down at the table. It appeared she was attempting to formulate a response. When she glanced up, she shot a look at him before she focused on Jeremiah. "The company I work for is a lab. Actually, they had a couple of complaints from the surrounding area about contaminated water. They sent me here to get some samples we can test and know for sure, so we can tell the county."

"We are on well water. Ours doesn't come from the county."

"I understand that, but if there are contaminants in the soil, it might be a problem with your water too. The Bandera County River Authority and Groundwater District is concerned about the area, from what I've been told."

He didn't like the sound of this at all. Why would the county be worried about them if they were on well water?

"I don't know the details. All I know is I am here to get some samples." She shifted her gaze around the table. "I'm not here to hurt anyone or do anything to jeopardize your operation."

"We didn't think you were, honey." His mother patted her hand. "Did we, boys?"

The murmur of agreement went around the table and he saw Rose physically relax.

"Thank you. I appreciate the backing."

The rest of the meal went by without any more confrontations, but he saw Jeff watching Rose very closely. It bothered him that his brother was suspicious of Rose, but then again, he was becoming more wary of her as well.

After they were finished, he walked Rose back to her cabin. "I need to finish up some work with that mare. Will you be okay by yourself until supper?"

She smiled and laid her palm against his cheek. "Yes, Joseph. I have some work I need to do as well. I might go ahead and run over to your neighbor's place to see if I can get the samples I need since they don't care for you. I wouldn't want you to get shot at again."

He frowned as she turned toward the cabin door and unlocked it.

When she turned back to face him, she said, "Oh, something strange happened earlier. After you'd left to get your clothes, I heard my door open and then close. I thought it was you returning already, but when you didn't come into the bathroom I looked out into the bedroom. There wasn't anyone there."

"I don't like you leaving your door unlocked."

"You were coming right back. I didn't think anything of it."

"Make sure you lock it when you're in there by yourself. It is usually safe on the ranch, but there is always the potential for problems. We do have other ranch hands besides my brothers and me."

"Didn't you say you had ghosts on the place?"

"Supposedly, yes."

"Hmm. I'm going to do some digging if you don't mind. I love the thought of ghosts, and I would love to see if I can find out some information."

"That'd be fine. All of us boys have thought about doing some research, but no one has had the time."

"Well, let me see what I can find. I might go into town too. Is there a library there?"

"Yeah. They should have old newspapers or books or something you can look at."

"Great." She reached up and kissed him on the lips, her mouth lingering for a hot second before she stepped back. "I'll see you at supper."

He turned on his heels and headed for the barn. The mare awaited him and he needed to finish getting her broke. It wasn't a simple process. It took weeks to properly train a horse to trail ride, especially getting one gentle enough where an inexperienced rider could be on it. They had a lot of horses on the place, many who were very gentle, but this little mare was kind of special. He'd picked her out himself on a trip to Houston a few months ago. She was a spotted saddle mare and had gorgeous markings. A white blaze ran down her nose and she had chestnut colored spots over most of her body along with lots of white.

The cooler interior felt good against the spring heat of the day. Some of the horses in the barn nickered at him as he made his way to the back and out to the paddock area where the mare had been stabled. He'd left her munching on some hay while he'd gone to eat. She lifted her head and gave him a bored look before going back to the small pile still left on the ground.

First things first. He needed to start with the halter. The one he was going to use hung over the fence post.

He grabbed the polyester rigging and approached her slowly, talking in small words and soothing tones as he moved. "Hey, pretty girl."

The mare eyed him warily.

"Easy, baby."

He held the halter in his right hand while he eased his left hand over the top of her head. She skittered away, side-stepping him as he continued to move closer every time she moved away.

Breaking a horse was a dance of sorts. It took a lot of patience and work.

He glanced to his right, noticing Jacob standing at the fence with his boot on the bottom railing and his arms dangling over the top. *Hmm.*

Without taking his eyes off the mare, he said, "Somethin' I can do for you, Jacob?"

"Nope."

"Don't you have somewhere to be?"

"Nope."

He liked his brothers, all of them, but Jacob was kind of special to him. There had been some hard times for his brother while he dealt with some personal issues. When he'd found his wife Paige, Joey had been the first one there with congratulations. In fact, one night he and a couple of the others had thought it would be a good idea to kidnap Paige and bring her to the ranch. Jacob had been in a particularly bad mood so they thought it would be funny to bring her home for his brother. They had been pretty drunk at the time, but it really had been hilarious when she met them at the top of her stairs with a shotgun, a mean dog, and a threat to blow holes through all of them.

"I'm sure Paige is looking for you right about now."

Jacob pulled his hat down lower on his forehead. "Not really. She's busy with the kids."

"So you decided to come hang out at the paddock with me? I'm touched."

"Actually, I'm curious about you and this redhead you've been hanging with."

"Rose?"

"Yep."

"Why?"

"She seems nice enough."

"But?"

"I'm concerned with her gathering these samples she's talking about."

"And?"

"What if something comes up in them to hurt the ranch? We could all lose our livelihood here. I mean for some of us, this is all we know, like you."

He contemplated that thought a lot longer than he probably needed to, but it bothered him nonetheless. He didn't know anything beyond ranching, horses, and cattle. If this wasn't here anymore, he wouldn't know what to do. College had never appealed to him although he could probably go back for agriculture or something along those lines. "It'll be fine."

"You're sure?"

"Hell no, Jacob! I don't fucking know anything, but I can't think about that. It's out of our hands if there is something here. I don't think Rose is out to hurt us though."

"I don't think so either. I can't help being concerned though, Joey. Do you know who the company is she's working for?"

"No. I haven't known her that long."

Jacob shifted so his other boot was on the rung of the rail. "Can you find out? Maybe we need to do a little digging of our own to find out what is going on."

He managed to get the halter over the mares head and hook it around her ears. He ran his hand over her nose, calming her even though her coat still twitched from nervousness. His palm slid down her side, smoothing the hair while he thought about Rose and what having her on the ranch could mean for the family. As much as he liked her, family came first. "I'll see what I can find out, Jacob. I wish I knew more about what she's talking about with these things."

"I'm sure. It's confusing with all this chemical stuff."

"You aren't kidding." He led the mare toward the fence. "Do you know what Jeremiah was talking about with this company he mentioned?"

"No. You know how he is. He's got his hands in so many different things, I'm not sure he even knows what they all are."

"That's true. He did mention a company by name and Rose got a funny look on her face. She asked to leave right after that."

Jacob ran his hand along his chin. "Where is she now?"

"She went into town. She said she had some work to do, and she needed to go by the Marshall's place to get a sample from there."

"Well, I guess there isn't anything more we can go right now. You do need to see if you can get the name of the company she words for though."

"I'll see what I can do."

"Okay." Jacob stepped back, dropping his booted foot to ground. "I'll see you at supper."

"Yep."

As his brother walked away, Joey wondered how he was going to go about getting the information about Rose's employer. He didn't want to make her suspicious or anything since he had no idea what they would do with the information once they had it.

He probably needed to talk to Jeremiah too. Rose's reaction when he mentioned the company's name was weird. She's gone pale and started to shake before she asked to leave in a hurry.

With the mare following close behind, he took her inside the barn and put her in a stall. He would work with her more tomorrow and see if he could actually get a saddle on her. Right now, he had some digging to do.

Chapter Twelve

Rose closed the newspaper she had opened on the huge table in the middle of the library. After she folded the paper, she sat back in her chair and thought about all she'd learned over the last several hours.

She'd gathered quite a bit of information on Thunder Ridge, its past inhabitants, and some of the colorful history of the area. She found that the ranch had been a working cattle ranch for quite some time, over one hundred years to be exact. After the Civil War, the area became a staging area for the Western Trail bringing along cowboys and settlers alike, including women of the night.

Some of those women took up residence at Thunder Ridge or what Thunder Ridge used to be a long time ago.

She gathered from the information that the main lodge that stood there now used to, in part, be the place where the women would take men upstairs to entertain. The lower level was for gambling and drinking mostly for the local cowboys before they went on long trail rides.

She had names of people who had been killed on the property including a couple of cowboys, a lady of the night, and three women who'd came west with their husbands to help settle the area, with their children. She didn't know all the details of what ghosts were seen or heard out there, but she was definitely intrigued by the stories she'd read in the newspapers at the library.

When a series of floods wiped out a lot of the local area in the early 1900s, the area became almost inaccessible. In the 1930s, the area became known for taking in guests at the local ranches offering camping, rodeos, dance halls, and fun for everyone.

She didn't know when Joseph's family had bought the ranch other than when the two older boys were little. By her calculations, that would have been about thirty years earlier, give or take, fairly recently by Old West standards.

The town itself had been established back in the mid-1850s.

History fascinated her, so this was right up her alley. She loved hearing about how the cattle trails went through, how the ranches were established usually by generations and generations of families, and the landscape had changed over the years.

"I'm sorry, ma'am, but the library is closing."

"Oh. Thank you. I hadn't realized how late it had gotten. I appreciate you letting me look through all these old newspapers."

The elderly woman glanced down at her notes. "You are doing some research on Thunder Ridge?"

"Yes, ma'am. I'm staying out there, and I've become friends with some of the family."

"You know about the ghosts, right?"

"I've heard that, yes. I was researching who lived out there and who might have died out there so I could help them learn something about the spirits they have on the place."

"The only one I know anything about is the old cowboy they've said they have seen. His name is Charlie Wilcom or that's what us locals believe. He'd been a ranch hand on the place when the ranch was built by the original owners. They had a big cattle ranch back then. Several thousand acres. From what I hear, he was trampled during a stampede during one of the rides. The description I've heard from the family fits the small picture we have of some cowboys here in the library."

"Can I see it?"

"Certainly." The woman led her down a long hallway toward the back of the library where several old pictures and artifacts were displayed. "This is a picture of several cowboys from that timeframe in front of the court house." She pointed to one man standing on the edge of the group.

Rose leaned closer to the picture to bring the man's face more into focus. *Interesting looking man.* When she stepped back, the librarian smiled. "I wonder if the family knows this picture is here?"

"You know, I'm not sure."

"I will definitely share this information with them as well as the other things I've learned." She held out her hand to shake the woman's. "I appreciate you helping me with this."

"It's nice to see young people interested in the local history. Not too many are these days." The woman tilted her head to the side. "If you don't mind me asking, where are you from? You don't have a Texas accent."

"I'm from New York. I came down here for work and met a local guy. His family owns the ranch, and I told him I would look into some of the history while I was in town today."

"Ah, yes. The Young family. Nice people." She laughed. "Those boys have been an important part of this town for a long time. They are all grown now and having families of their own."

"Yes, they are."

The clock in the corner bonged loudly on the hour. "Well, time for this old woman to go home. It was very nice talking to you, miss?"

"My name is Rose Gilbert."

"Pretty name."

"Thank you."

"I hope to see you around here again some time."

"I appreciate it, but probably not. I will be going back to New York in a few days."

"Ah." She shook her head. "Pity." A smile lifted the corners of her mouth. "But then again, one of those Young brothers might catch your eye and you'll stay for a while."

Rose couldn't help but smile in return. "Maybe." She moved back to the table to gather her bag. "Thank you again for helping me. I appreciate your time."

"Not a problem, young lady."

"Goodbye."

"Goodbye."

Rose went through the doors as the woman locked it behind her. She glanced first one way and then the other down the streets of Bandera. The town itself seemed quaint, somewhere she would enjoy wiling the day away beneath a nice tree as she sipped something cold. For tonight though, she needed to do some more digging. The information she'd received on Thunder Ridge was intriguing, and she hoped the family would be interested in it.

After she approached her car and slid inside, she took a moment to check her cell phone for messages. She'd had it shut off in the library. Once the cell phone tower connected, she got a beep indicating a message.

When she punched the voicemail button, she heard her boss's voice. "Rose, I need you to call me immediately. The county is pushing for results on those samples. They want them as soon as possible."

The county? Somehow, I don't think it's the county wanting these yesterday.

She started her car to head back out to the ranch. It was almost supper time. Her job was finished. Everything had been collected. *Now what am I going to do? Going home seemed so distant a few days ago, but now that it is looming in the next couple of days, I don't want to go.*

The samples she retrieved from the Marshall's place sat in her bag in the backseat. The old man seemed suspicious of her when she'd approached their door earlier, which was understandable. They probably didn't have too many visitors from New York around this area.

She also got a glimpse of Jessica. The girl was gorgeous with long dark hair, big brown eyes, a nice straight smile, and thin. She could have been a model. Rose didn't like the feelings stirring in her heart when she thought of the girl with Joseph. Not knowing whether the two had ever had sex for sure, all she could imagine was the two of them twisted up in the sheets having wild, passionate sex. Her stomach knotted at the thought.

Barbed wire fences zipped past her window as she drove down the paved road. Out here in Hill Country, there wasn't much other than ranches scattered here and there, junipers, Bluebonnets, cattle, and an occasional sighting of wildlife. Life here would be simple—work hard, love harder, and cherish the little things. In New York, her life was hustle and bustle from the time the sun came up until she went to bed exhausted at the end of the day. You never really had time for yourself.

She pulled into the driveway of the ranch, pressed in the code, and watched as the gate slowly slid open. Longhorn cattle grazed in the distance, periodically bawling to each other.

Sound.

It was something that was part of everyday life in New York.

In Texas silence surrounded a person. Other than the buzz of a bee, rattle of horse tack, or the laughter of a child, the quiet solitude of the ranch enveloped you in the simplicity of ranch life.

When she pulled her car up in front of her little cabin, she pushed the gearshift into park and shut it off. Her gaze focused on the bushes in front of her car. *How in the hell am I going to get out of this with work? I'm afraid they are going to rig the results, causing the ranch to have to close so the drilling company can buy it cheap. If I tell the family the truth, they are going to think I had something to do with this.*

Her phone jiggled and as she looked at the screen, she cussed under her breath. It was her boss. She had to answer it or he would continue to call.

"Hello?"

"Did you get my message earlier, Rose? I need those samples."

"I have them done. I will FedEx them tomorrow. You should have them the day after."

"Excellent. The investors…uh, I mean the county is harping on me for those samples."

Fucker. He's totally in on this. "I understand."

"Good, good. I will talk to you as soon as I have the samples. Plan on being back in the office Monday morning."

"Yes, sir."

He hung up the phone without even a goodbye. *This whole thing just stinks of corruption. But what the hell do I do about it?*

* * * *

Joey watched Rose walk through the door to the main lodge, drinking her in as she came closer. She was a beautiful woman and one he'd been growing fonder of as they spent more time together.

If he really thought about it, he could say she'd become an important part of his life in a very short time, but what to do with that information.

"Joseph."

"Hey, babe." He pulled out the chair next to him for her. "We should be eating soon, but as a guest you can go on up there if you want."

"No, it's okay. I'll wait for you and the family."

"How was your day, Rose?" Nina asked from across the table.

All eyes focused on Rose. "It's was productive. I found out some interesting information on the ranch for you all, concerning the ghosts and the history."

"Oh?" His dad picked up his glass of iced tea and took a drink. "Tell us about it."

"I was going to wait until everyone was served their meal, but I got some great stuff at the library and the librarian even gave me some insight." He retrieved a glass for her, sitting it down by her plate. "Thank you, Joseph."

"You're welcome."

"Anyway, as you probably know, this was a working cattle ranch for over one hundred years. The whole area was part of the Western Trail, and this property was a big contributor to that."

The few guests staying on the ranch had filled their plates and took their seats.

Nina indicated the family could be served now as everyone climbed to their feet to get their food.

Once the group took their places again, Rose continued. "There was also a brothel here, in this very house. The rooms upstairs were used for the ladies of the night while the main rooms were used for gambling, drinking, and so forth." She glanced at him. "Didn't you say you have a cowboy ghost here?"

"Yeah."

"From my research, I got a name and I also saw a picture of him in the library. I haven't seen him myself so I don't know for sure it's the same guy, but the librarian seemed pretty sure. His name is Charlie Wilcom. From what I understand, he was trampled in a stampede during a trail drive. He'd been a ranch hand on the place from the time of the original owners."

"What else did you learn, Rose?" His mom tilted her head to the side as she focused on what Rose was saying.

"There wasn't anything concrete on anyone being killed during the brothel days. I did get some information saying there were three women and some children that had come west to meet up with one's husband who had come earlier. There was apparently a fire here that took their lives in a house that had sat back on the hill behind the cabins. It was a grandmother, mother, and sister along with several children."

"Wow." Jeff had set his fork down and was completely intrigued by the information. "That's more than any of us have been able to find out for quite some time. Good job, Rose."

"Thank you. Actually, it was a lot of fun. I love history and this gave me the opportunity to explore it. I appreciate you all letting me dig into the past of your property." Joey reached under the table, squeezing her fingers to let her know he was proud of her. "I wish I would have been able to learn more."

The conversation changed directions as everyone began eating in earnest.

James cleared his throat. "Joey, did you get that mare broke today?"

"Yes, Dad, I did or partially broke. I got the halter on her. She seems very sweet, and I think she'll make a great addition to the herd."

"Excellent."

Chatter flowed around him as he thought about the ranch, his job, and what the whole thing meant to him. His talk with Jacob earlier had bothered him all day and he hadn't been able to get it out of his thoughts. If something were to happen with this place, his whole life would change. Several of his brothers would have the same problem without a secondary career to fall back on. True, most of the wives in the group had a career that would sustain them for a while, but their long term future would be in jeopardy.

Jeremiah spoke up. "I've done some more digging on the drilling in the area and I think we need to seriously contemplate having our property tested for oil."

James turned to face him. "I'm not sure that is a good idea, Jeremiah. I know it could possibly set the entire family up for life, but it might also be detrimental to our setup."

"I've been in contact with the drilling company. If we give them the okay, they'll be out within days to test."

"This needs to be a family vote, I think," Nina added. "We don't want one person to go off on a tangent that might hurt the family as a whole."

"I agree, sweetheart, but let's leave this discussion for another time when we don't have guests close by. This is a family topic, not something we need to be sharing with the public."

"Of course, James."

Topics turned to the cattle operation, what would be happening for the next week, and guests that would be arriving to stay.

Darkness descended over the ranch as dinner concluded and everyone went their separate ways for the evening. He knew his brothers would be off with their spouses and kids, his parents would retire to their private quarters for the night, and Rose would probably go to her cabin. *Would it be better to follow her in a bit or go with her now?* Thoughts of being with her this evening had been driving him nuts all day. He wanted her, there was no doubt about that, but maybe he should let her be tonight. They had been together almost constantly since they'd met. Some might misconstrue that to be a relationship, which it wasn't. Relationships were for people who lived near each other, could be together all the time, and had thoughts of the future, right?

Right.

"Joseph?"

"Yeah?" She ran her fingernail down the front of his shirt along the row of buttons.

"Are you going to join me tonight in my cabin?"

"Do you want me to?"

Lust sparkled in her gaze. "Of course."

"I thought maybe you might want to have a night to yourself."

"I'd much rather have you."

"I aim to please."

"That you do, cowboy, that you do." She took his hand in hers, guiding him out the door of the lodge, down the path to her cabin, and then through the door after she'd unlocked it.

When she closed it behind them, he pushed her against the dark panel of wood behind her as he brought their mouths close, but not touching. Their breaths mingle as he stared into her eyes. Desire raged in her gaze, dilating her pupils until they almost encompassed her entire iris. Her breasts were crushed against his chest. One knee parted her thighs. Her heat scorched his leg were it rested against her center.

With one wrist in each hand, he kept her pinned to the door. His heart hammered in his chest, pounding against his ribs. He brushed his lips against hers in a slow, tempting taste, barely resisting crushing their mouths together in a frantic meeting.

His hard-on felt like it was drilling a hole in his pants. Desperate need clawed at his insides to be buried inside her sweet heat soon. "I need you, Rose."

"Take me. Make me yours."

Unable to resist her pull, he took what he desired more than anything in the world right at this moment.

He picked her up, so she could wrap her legs around his waist, and moved toward the big bed next to the wall. When he released her from his hold, she slid down his body in an unhurried move that drove him crazy.

Her top came off with a tug of the material over her head, revealing her naked breasts to his gaze. She hadn't worn a bra today under her tank top. Her nipples were already pulled into tight little nubs that just begged for his mouth. He cupped each one in his palms before rubbing his thumbs over the tips.

A groan spilled from her lips as she tilted her head back on her shoulders. "More."

He took the right one in his mouth, sucking hard as she grabbed his head and held it to her breast. The mounds were perfect, pink tipped, and deliciously hard against his tongue.

Her knees gave out as she sank to the bed and laid back. He followed her down, loving how she moaned softly and tossed her head from side to side. *So responsive.*

He moved his left hand to the button at her waist, flicking it open with his fingers so he could touch her. The heat of her pussy scalded him as he slipped his fingers beneath her panties. She was hot enough to sear him.

One finger glanced off her clit, bringing her hips surging up. "God, Joseph. Please touch me."

Gathering a little bit of her juices on his fingers, he rubbed her clit in a circular motion first fast, and then slow. He wanted to drive her wild.

She tossed her head as she moaned deep in her throat, her fists pulling at the bedspread beneath her hands.

He moved around so he could pull off her jeans and panties, exposing her to his gaze. The sight of her open, glistening pussy drove him beyond crazy. The need to taste her had him panting like he'd run a hundred miles at top speed.

Two fingers spread her open for him as she offered herself. Her clit was puffy and pink, peeking out from under the hood. Cream glittered from where it had been smeared on her thighs. The tangy scent of her passion reached his nose as he settled himself between her thighs. He loved the smell of her. With his nose buried in the crease of her thigh, he inhaled, taking it in so he could savor it knowing he put it there.

He flattened his tongue, licking her from slit to clit in one long stroke. The taste of her drove his desire higher.

Her hips bucked against the mattress as she groaned softly. "Yes, please, more."

Using only the tip of his tongue, he flicked the nub of her clit quickly, knowing he would drive her to an explosive climax quickly if he continued.

He slowed the battering of her senses, letting her come down a little before he drove her back up. Over and over he brought her almost to the edge without letting her come.

"Joseph, God please let me come. I hurt so bad," she begged softly.

"Since you asked so nicely, I will give you what you want." He flicked her clit several times as he drove two fingers into her grasping channel. The walls of her vagina clamped down on him as she exploded in a climax, shouting his name loud enough they probably heard her at the main lodge. He didn't care.

He quickly shed his clothes, dropping everything to the floor in a pile after he toed off his boots, and then settled himself between her parted thighs. The head of his cock bumped at her opening before he slowly pushed inside of her hot center. "You feel so good."

"Fuck me, Joseph. Please."

Thrust after thrust, he drove his cock deeper. The heat of her burned him clear to his soul, imprinting her there. He would never be the same after Rose.

Chapter Thirteen

Two days later she stood near her car where it was parked next to her cabin, touching the front of Joseph's shirt with her fingertips. Letting go had never been so hard.

"You'll call me when you get home?" he asked in a whisper.

"Yes, but it will be late this evening."

"It's okay. I'm usually up late."

She leaned her forehead against his chin. The thought of leaving him, this place, was like a hot poker to her chest. Her heart ached with the need to stay, but that wasn't possible. Her life, her job, her family—everything was in New York. "I wish I didn't have to go." She choked back a small sob, trying desperately not to cry.

He kissed her head and pulled her tighter to his chest. "I'm gonna miss you."

"Don't. Please. This is hard enough."

"It's true."

Tears came in earnest as she desperately tried to wipe them away with the back of her hand.

He took over the chore, kissing them away with his lips. "Maybe I can come and visit sometime."

"Sure. You're welcome anytime. I hope you know that."

"Thank you." She sniffed, wiped her nose, and stepped out of his embrace. "I'd better go. My plane leaves in three hours."

He opened her car door and waited for her to slide inside before shutting it behind her. She rolled the window down so she could touch him one last time. "Thank you for everything."

"No thanks needed."

"Yes, there is. You've made the time here very special for me, Joseph, and I will always treasure it, more than you know."

He cleared his throat before he said, "I've grown rather fond of you, Rose. I hope you know that."

She pressed her lips together as she tried to fight the smile that wanted to break free. It didn't work. "I really like you too, Joseph." *Say it! Tell him you love him!* "You have a special place in my heart."

"You should probably go."

"Yeah, I should."

"Safe travels."

"I'll call you later tonight."

He tapped on the top of her car as she rolled the window back up and waved a little goodbye.

The long driveway out of Thunder Ridge seemed like it took forever, but not long enough as fresh tears scalded her cheeks, blurring her vision as she tried to blink them away. God help her she did love him. *How in the hell can I fall in love with someone in such a short time?* "Easy when it's Joseph."

Her chest ached with the need to go back, to tell him she loved him, and see where things might go from there, but she couldn't. Everything she had was in New York, and walking away from it all for someone she wasn't even sure returned her feelings seemed ludicrous.

"No. Right now, I have things I need to do in New York. I'll keep in touch with him and we'll see what happens. If he cares about me like I care about him, then things will work out. I have to believe that."

The drive to San Antonio dragged on forever, or so it seemed. She returned her rental car, took the bus to the terminal, and then checked-in for her flight. A quick glance at the watch on her wrist told her she had about two hours before flight time. After she went through security, she slowly walked down the long terminal searching for her gate. When she found it, she spied an empty seat next to the wall, opened her phone, and checked her messages.

None.

Her life seemed so empty now without Joseph and his family. What did she have to look forward to? Her parents lived across town from her in New York, Brandt had moved out of their apartment when she'd broken up with him, instead of her needing her father to pick up her stuff, and she didn't have a ton of friends.

Work would be waiting when she got there in the morning. She needed to report first thing to her boss on her trip to Texas. The samples she'd sent should already been through processing, and she wanted to see the reports.

Deciding to try to get her mind off the here and now, she opened Mesa's book she had in her carryon. It was the same one she'd started on the trip out there, but now it seemed so much more real to her. She could see the faces of the cowboys as if they stood in front of her. Funny thing was, they all looked like the Young brothers.

Before she knew it, it was time to board. The flight home would be several hours, including a plane change. She hoped she could sleep. It would help her forget for a short time anyway.

When she took her seat onboard, she really hoped she wouldn't get some talkative older woman next to her. Talking wasn't high on her list right now. She just wanted to be left alone to wallow in her misery.

A woman about seventy asked, "Is this seat taken?"

"No, ma'am."

"Thank you."

"You're welcome." Rose tried to look out the window to discourage talk, but it didn't work.

"What beautiful hair you have."

Rose glanced back at the woman and said, "Thank you." She smiled before sliding her purse under the seat in front of her. "Are you headed home?"

"Yes, ma'am."

"Did you have a good time in Texas?"

"Yes, I did. I spent the better part of it out in Bandera at a fantastic guest ranch."

"Which one? I live out near Bandera."

"It's called Thunder Ridge."

The older woman clapped her hands. "Oh yes! Nina, James, and the boys. I've been friends with that family for a number of years. My husband used to go with them to auctions all the time."

"Do you own a ranch as well?"

"Oh no. My Bill just loved cattle, horses, and ranching, but we never owned one ourselves. Too much work for us old folks, but James and the boys were very kind to him, letting him go with them for the experience. We had a small piece of property not far from Thunder Ridge. The boys always came over to look in on us. They are such nice boys."

"Yes, they are. Are you headed to New York for vacation?"

"No. I'm going to visit our daughter and her family. My husband died last year and I haven't seen them since the funeral."

"Oh, I'm so sorry."

"Thank you, honey, but its fine." She reached over and patted Rose's hand. "We had sixty-three years together and he lived a long, happy life. He was eighty-nine when he passed."

The plane pushed back from the gate and was in the air before she knew it. "Where does your daughter live?"

"Not far from Central Park on West 77th Street."

"That's amazing. I have a small apartment on 78th Street."

"Really? How fascinating. Such a small world."

"When were you in New York last?"

"It's been several years. Bill wasn't well for quite a while before he died, so we couldn't travel much. My daughter would come to us." The flight attendant came by to ask what they wanted to drink and to hand them peanuts. "So not like it used to be. I can remember when you used to get a full meal on these flights."

Rose smiled. She really liked this woman. "I hope you have a good time with your daughter and family."

"I'm sure I will. It's been pretty quiet at home without my husband and with no other family in the area, I don't get out much. I'm thinking of selling the property and moving to New York to be close to her."

"I'm sure you would be able to sell it easy enough."

"Maybe. It's a nice place with some good pasture land even though it hasn't been ranched for a very long time. Nina's boys would come over and hay it for us every year."

"Sounds nice."

"Listen to me. I've talked your ear off for over thirty minutes and I don't even know your name."

"It's Rose."

"What a beautiful name and it fits you perfectly." Her eyes twinkled as she glanced over at Rose. "Mine is Milly Henderson."

"It's nice to meet you, Milly."

The flight attendant brought their drinks and they settled into their seats to enjoy them.

"So which of the boys were you spending time with while you were at Thunder Ridge? I believe the only one not attached these days is Joseph."

Rose grinned. "It was Joseph."

"I should have guessed, even if he is the only one available these days. He's a sweet boy. Very handsome too."

"Yes, he is."

"Just my observation, but he would be a nice catch for you, Rose."

She chuckled. "I'm sure he would, Milly, but I don't live in the area, remember?"

"Yes, but wouldn't you like to live in Texas? It's a beautiful place."

"It is, that's true."

"I can see you've thought about it."

"I won't lie, yes I have, but there are things that would prevent that from happening. One is my job."

"What do you do?"

"I'm a microbiologist."

"Well now, that's an impressive title."

"Yes it is, but it also makes working outside of a larger area a bit more difficult."

"Tell me what you love about New York?"

"It's great having everything so close by, shops, restaurants, museums, or the park. You can get anywhere pretty quickly by subway. The seasons are seasons with snow in the winter, warm summers, beautiful falls, and green springs. My family is close."

"Now what do you not like about the city?"

"The crime. Too many people. Noise. Close neighbors. Smog. Traffic."

"What was the one thing you noticed about Bandera that made an impression on you?"

"The quiet. I could hear myself think out there." She inhaled a long, deep breath and glanced out the window as she rubbed the spot above her heart. It ached right now, something fierce. When she turned back toward Milly, she could see the woman's piercing gaze on her.

"You left there a few hours ago. What do you miss already about being there?"

With her lips pressed together, she fought the tears burning her eyes before she whispered, "Joseph."

"I think you should tell him when you get home. He probably would like to hear that."

"Maybe." She exhaled a big breath. "I don't think he feels the same."

"I bet he does. I've known those boys a long time, him especially since he's the baby, and I can tell you one thing about him, when he falls, he will fall hard. He loves his family fiercely and when he picks the one girl he wants to spend the rest of his life with, he won't let go."

"Thank you, Milly. I'll think about it. There is something I need to clear up with my employer before I can think to my future, and it might affect things with him on a really bad level."

"I'm sure everything will work out as it should. Keep the faith, Rose. If it is meant to be, it will be."

* * * *

Jeremiah handed Joseph the report they had received from the county that morning. The whole family was gathered in the main lodge to discuss what this meant. He read the words, his heart sinking into the pit of his stomach like a rock.

Conversation buzzed around him like a thousand bees on the trail of pollen in the spring. The one thing that registered in his brain was the mention of Rose.

"She had to know. She's the one who got the samples. They probably told her days ago, even before she left." Jeff paced the room, running his hands through his hair. "I knew we shouldn't have trusted her here."

"Jeff, you can't blame Rose. She was doing her job," Nina said from her spot on the couch.

"Bullshit! I bet they called her the minute they got the results, and she hit the pavement on the run so she wouldn't have to fuckin' face any of us."

Rose had left five days before to return to New York and it had seemed very fast. One minute she was there and the next she had to go back.

All eyes focused on him. "What? I didn't know anything about this."

"You brought her here, Joey."

"She would have come even if I hadn't. It was her job to get the samples. I didn't know about it before she came out, but she would have anyway."

"You were sleepin' with her," Joel replied. "You didn't suspect anything?"

"Like fuckin' her had anything to do with her job, Joel."

James raised his voice so he could be heard above the rapidly rising noise. "Enough, boys. That kind of talk is best not done here in front of the women and children."

"I, for one, want to know what's going on, Dad," Mesa said as she kept a close eye on her kids running around the couches. "This affects all of us."

"She's right." Peyton, Paige, Callie, Candace, Mandy, Samantha, and Terri all nodded in agreement. "We are all in this together, whatever happens."

"James, what exactly does the paper say?" Nina climbed to her feet and approached Joey where he stood still holding the paper tightly in his hands. "Let me see." He watched his mother scan the document before she turned to face the group. "Apparently there was a complaint filed with the county saying our water has been contaminated and they brought in an out-of-state lab to test the samples. The county has been given information on the water and soil samples taken from our property and tested by Reece Labs in New York City." She turned and looked him in the eye. "I'm assuming this is the company that Rose worked for?"

"I guess. I never asked."

She placed her hand on his cheek. "This is not your fault, Joey."

"I know."

She glanced down at the paper again. "This letter says that due to the quality of the water on the property and potential health hazards to the guests and people living on the land, we either have to totally redig the wells to check for contamination, or we have to close the ranch."

The room exploded in a roar of sound. Everyone talked at once, shouting over each other to try to be heard. He didn't understand what this all meant, but he knew it wasn't good. Needing a moment to himself, he turned on his heels, walked through the dining area and went outside. The sun beat down on his head as he walked toward the barn, his solace in the crazy world Thunder Ridge had become.

What the hell would they do if they had to close and move? This was their home, the only home they had ever known. True, his parents had enough money they could move somewhere else, but if the property was uninhabitable they wouldn't be able to sell it for anything.

He approached the stall where they kept the wheelbarrow and shovel for cleaning out the stalls. Hard work never hurt anyone and it would give him a task to do to keep his mind numb. *Mom and Dad will figure this out, they have to.*

After several minutes, he heard boots on the dirt coming toward him. When he turned to see who it was, he wasn't surprised to see Jeremiah. "What's up?"

"I figured this is where you would be."

"I needed to get out of there. It was getting crazy."

"Yeah, I know. It's not much better yet. Jeff is yelling, of course, and everyone else is trying to figure out what we do from here."

"What do we do, Jeremiah? If the water is bad, we won't be able to sell if we have to close."

"No, we won't. I'm in contact with the oil drilling company though. They still want to drill."

"At what cost though? Are they willing to buy the property with bad water?"

"They don't care about water quality, but the big thing is, the property isn't worth near as much in mineral rights this way."

"So we have to sell the rights for a lot less than we would have before? Less money to divide up."

"Yeah."

"This stinks to high heaven."

"I know."

"What do we do for now?"

"We have to close the ranch until we see what our options are. I don't think we have a lot though."

"It doesn't sound like it."

"I'm going to tell everyone that I've set up a meeting with the drilling company for one week from today to see what their offer is. Until then, we can't take guests."

Joey exhaled as he rested on the shovel's handle. Work still needed to be done. Animals still needed to be cared for.

The world still went around even if it seemed their lives were about to get turned upside down. "Want me to come back in?"

"Yeah. You need to be there too."

"All right. I'll be there in a sec. Let me dump this load."

"Things will work out. We'll be okay as long as we stick together as a family."

"I know."

"See you in a minute."

Joey watched his brother's slumped shoulders as he headed back toward the main lodge. His gut told him something wasn't right, but he didn't know what and for some reason it had a lot to do with Rose.

All eyes focused on him when he came through the door. Being the center of attention made him uncomfortable on his best day. Today, it felt even worse.

He took a seat at one of the tables as Jeremiah took a spot at the head of the room under where Clyde, Thunder Ridge's first longhorn bull, hung above the fireplace.

"All right. This is what I need to tell you all. Please, hold any questions until I'm done. Mission Drilling has been in contact with me again today. They want to come out to talk with us in a week, to give us some information on an offer for the property, I assume. Knowing what I know, their offer will be significantly less than what it was before for the drilling rights. With the water containments here on the property, we won't be able to sell as a working ranch any longer, if that's what we had thought to do. As it stands, we will have to shut down to guests until we figure out what we are doing. It's probably not even safe for any of us to be on the property."

"I'm not leaving. This is my home." His mom stood straight and tall as she stood by the window with her arms across her chest. "I don't care what they say. I'm not leaving."

Several of the others shouted their agreement.

"Besides, most of us have our own homes on this land. If the water in Thunder Ridge's wells are bad, ours probably are too." Jason had his arm around his wife as Peyton snuggled into his embrace.

"Then I think we are all in this together. We will stay until we can at least talk to the drilling company next week, and then we came make a decision," Jeremiah concluded as he pulled Callie up next to him. "You all know I will do everything I can to secure a future for this family, even if it takes every dime I have in the bank. I will never turn my back on any one of you."

All of them disbursed to take care of the things needing their attention as Joey wandered back to the barn. He wanted to call Rose, but he knew right now she was probably at work. Did she really know about this before she went home? Did she have anything to do with this whole thing? If so, why didn't she warn them?

His thoughts went back to their time spent together on the ranch making love, getting to know each other, and the way she'd wiggled herself into his heart before he'd ever even realized she was there.

For the last several days, they'd talk almost every night. She'd call when she got home from work and she would tell him about her day, how her cat was, what the weather was like in New York. Then she would tell him how much she missed his touch, his kiss, and the way he would make love to her.

He'd even made tentative plans to go out to see her in a couple of months, but now, he didn't know what to do. Had he misplaced his trust in her?

His cell phone jingled in his pocket. When he pulled it out, he saw it was Rose on the phone. Not sure what to say to her at this point in time, he let it go to voicemail, and returned it to his pocket. Maybe later he would call her back. Right now, he didn't know what to think. His heart told him to trust in his feelings for her, but his head said she had something to do with this mess. Love wasn't always the right answer.

Chapter Fourteen

One solid week. She hadn't talk to him in seven days and here she was on a damned plane to Texas.

The reports had come in on Thunder Ridge's samples over a week ago and rather than try to explain anything to the family, she'd tried talking to Joseph. He wouldn't answer her calls. Message after message had been left on his voicemail without one single return call.

This was bad, but good.

After she'd seen the report, she'd taken the last week to run her own tests on the samples. When she'd taken them in the first place, her gut feeling had been to keep a second set of samples in her own gear, and not send them to the lab with the others. Now she had the proof in her hands that the first set of samples had been tampered with.

She'd rerun the second set of tubes several times to check her results and every time they had come back clean, so why did the first ones contain contaminants? The only answer was tampering. The property had to appear so uninhabitable the family would have to sell to the drilling company at rock bottom prices.

The plane touched down in San Antonio minutes later. The second she had her bags in her hands, she was headed to the rental car company. Bandera was an hour drive. It would give her time to formulate her proof to present to the family. They had to believe her, they just had to.

What if they didn't? What if they all turned their backs on her, including Joseph?

I'll have to make sure he knows I love him and that I did what I could to protect him and his family.

Her hands gripped the steering wheel tight enough her knuckles turned white. "They have to understand."

Unable to stand the quiet, she turned on the radio, tapping her fingers along with the tune as she tried to focus on something besides how shit could hit the fan and she would be out on her ass if this didn't go down like she wanted it to. She'd quit her job in New York the instant she was positive the results had been tampered with, given notice at her apartment, and packed a bag to head back to Texas.

God help her if this blew up in her face.

When the gate slid open as she pulled up to it she had to take a deep breath to calm her nerves. She drove down the long driveway and parked her car, still unsure of how to approach this. She wanted to find Joseph first and explain things to him before they got the family together to try to sort this out, but other than the barn, she wasn't sure where he might be.

Deciding to go into the main lodge first since she'd checked the clock on the dash and found it to be almost supper time, she figured they might be there. She really didn't want to barge in on the meal, so she went around to the front of the lodge to go in through the main room.

As she pushed open the door, she heard voices.

"Mr. Young, this is a very lucrative offer we are making you on the drilling rights."

"It's a lot lower than the original offer you had shown Jeremiah."

"Yes it is, but because of the contaminated water, you won't be able to use the property for anything else before, during, or after drilling has ceased. The property is basically worthless without finding oil, which we aren't even positive exists."

Shit, am I too late? She moved inside quietly, not to alert anyone she was there. She wanted to hear what they were saying before she made her presence known.

"We understand that, Mr. Pritchard, but this is our home. This is all we know, and to ask us to basically give it up is not something we are willing to do without a fair price so we can move on and find something else."

"Dad, I think we should have the water and soil tested ourselves," Jonathan suggested.

Mr. Pritchard turned purple. "That would take weeks."

"We aren't in any hurry."

"As you know by the reports provided by Reece Labs out of New York your wells are contaminated with microorganisms that make your property uninhabitable. What we are proposing should make your family very comfortable for the foreseeable future."

Rose couldn't keep quiet any longer. She had the proof in her hands that what they said wasn't true. "Excuse me."

Twenty sets of eyes turned to her.

"Rose?" Joseph came toward her. "What are you doing here?"

Jeff stormed toward her. "Get her the fuck out of here! She doesn't belong on this property."

"Please, let me explain."

"There is nothing to explain." He grabbed her arm to shove her out, but Joseph stepped between them.

"Let her talk."

"I had to come, Joseph. I had to set things straight."

"What are you talking about?"

"The reports. They're wrong. They've been tampered with. There is nothing wrong with your water or soil. It's as clean as it needs to be for your family to continue to operate Thunder Ridge."

"What? How do you know?"

"I reran the tests myself after I saw the report. I've been trying to call you for a week to explain, but you wouldn't answer the phone."

His gaze dropped before coming back to hers. "I'm sorry."

"It's okay. I understand. I'm sure your whole family was upset."

"Yeah."

Mr. Pritchard stopped next to her. "Who the hell are you to question those results?"

"I am or was the lead microbiologist on this project. I suspected tampering so I did the tests myself on a second set of samples I kept on my person until I got them to the lab." She turned to Nina and James. "There is a connection between this drilling company and my former boss, Mr. Albright. He is a cousin of the owners of the drilling company. I believe they've been manipulating not just your family but several others as well so they could buy oil rich property for next to nothing, and make millions drilling it, leaving the land dry before they sell it." She held the report out to James. "As you can see, this shows normal flora in the water and soil. I've filed this new report with the county already, so you should be receiving a new letter from them in the next day or two, showing your property to be fine for habitation by your family and guests."

James stepped forward and took the report from her fingers. After he scanned it for several moments, he turned to their guest. "Mr. Pritchard, I believe you need to leave our property and take your proposal with you. Tell your partners or whoever you represent that Thunder Ridge is not for sale now nor will it ever be to the likes of you."

Rose grinned as the man huffed, grabbed his briefcase, and headed for the door.

Joseph had moved off by himself to her left as the conversation flowed around her. There were several questions from Nina and James as well as Jeremiah on what she'd learned and what they needed to do now to fix this whole thing.

Right now, she just wanted to talk to Joseph.

Nina moved to her side and said, "Rose, I hope you plan to stay here on Thunder Ridge at least for a day or two so we can properly thank you. It sounds as if you gave up your job for us, and for that we need to take care of you for at least a couple of days."

"I would appreciate it, Nina. I don't have a place to stay yet. I flew here as soon as I could in hopes of making things right."

Nina hugged her tight. "You did well, sweetie. I think you need to talk to Joey though. He's been torn about this whole thing."

She nodded as she stepped back. "I will right now."

When she made her way toward him, he wouldn't meet her gaze.

"Joseph?"

He glanced up and she was taken aback by the sadness in his eyes. She didn't know how to respond to that. Why was he sad? Had she hurt him in some way she wasn't aware of?

"Can we talk?"

"I suppose."

Nina shoved a key into her hand. "Here. Go on out to your cabin. It's quiet there."

Rose took his hand in hers and led him out the door. They walked in silence out to the cabin she'd used before, her heart pounding in her chest the whole way there. She wasn't sure what to say or do to fix whatever the problem was.

After she opened the door, she led him inside and shut it behind her before she turned to face him.

He stood in the middle of the room, his hands shoved in his pockets like he didn't know what to do with them. He looked so good to her, she wanted to eat him up, but first she needed him to hold her more than anything.

She took a step toward him. He looked up, meeting her gaze.

"I'm sorry, Joseph."

"You saved my family. You saved the ranch."

She shook her head. "I didn't do anything other than what was right. I should have said something before when I had suspicions. I'd done some research on the drilling company when Jeremiah mentioned them, but I didn't say anything. I found out then there was a connection between my boss and the drilling company."

He took a couple of steps toward her before shoving his hands in the hair by her ears so he could cradle her head. "God, I missed you."

The words were music to her ears. "I missed you too."

"Did you really quit your job?"

"Yes."

"What are you gonna do now?"

"I don't know. I thought I'd stay here for a few weeks. I kind of like being on the ranch."

"What about work? Your family? Your place in New York?"

"My parents are watching my apartment for now. I've already given them notice that I'm moving."

He frowned. "Where are you moving to?"

"I thought I'd find a place in San Antonio or something."

"Here?"

"Yeah, that is if you won't be too upset to have me close by."

"Baby, I'm more than happy to have you here. The closer the better." He pulled her to his chest. "In fact, this isn't quite close enough for me."

His whispered words against her mouth were a balm to her soul. He wanted her.

"Joseph?"

"Yeah?"

She took in a big breath and then said, "I love you."

When he leaned back, she wasn't sure he would answer until a grin spread across his lips. "I love you too."

"You do?"

"Yeah. I've been going crazy without you here. I've been impossible to live with not talking to you this past week. My brothers almost threw me out."

She giggled. "I can totally see them doing that."

"I really do love you."

Unable to wait any longer to have her mouth against his, she reached behind his head and brought his lips closer. "I need you to kiss me, but I want you to know I love you so much, my heart is full. You are everything to me."

He brought their mouths together in a slow, sensuous kiss before he let go of his passion and crushed their mouths together. Need exploded low in her belly. Her body trembled with everything running through her, wanting to be closer to this man. How, why, where she'd fallen in love with him, she didn't know, but she had. It was part of her, he was part of her, and she didn't want it to ever end. He'd become her life.

His hands skimmed down her back, pulling her in closer as he gripped her butt in his palms.

His lips moved along her jaw, nipping at the flesh until he reached her ear. His hot breath scalded her as he whispered, "I love you so much."

Tears pricked behind her eyelids. She never thought she'd hear those words from someone like him.

Milly's comment came back to her with sharp clarity. When he fell, he would fall hard, and love with all his heart. Apparently, he fallen for her, Rose, the strange woman from New York who'd blown into his life one early spring day.

"Why are you crying?" he asked, looking down into her eyes.

"Because I realize that you are a special man and for you to say you love me means everything."

"Darlin', I think I fell in love with you the day I met you. Seeing you sitting at the diner in the sun, your hair burning like it had a life of its own, sketching something as if you were in your own little world, and then you looked up and caught my gaze across the room. My heart literally stopped at that moment before it began to beat again with only a rhythm you and I can hear."

"You weren't alone."

"No, I wasn't, but right then, nothing else seemed to matter except finding out who you were."

"I saw you sitting there with your friend and the first thing I wondered about was if you were a real cowboy. You looked the part, but one never knows. Then when you stopped to talk to me, it was like my world centered."

"Don't we sound like two sappy lovebirds?"

"I know, right?"

His deep, rich laughter sent shivers along her arms.

"What do we do now, Joseph?"

"I'm not sure, darlin'. I've never been in love before."

"Me either, really. I thought I was, but it was nothing like this. These feelings for you are so raw, so powerful, I'm not sure how to handle it. The last week without you has been something I don't want to do again. I couldn't eat, I couldn't sleep, and trying to work seemed impossible."

He ran his fingertips down her cheek. "Stay here with me. We will figure out something. I need you with me."

She glanced down at his chest and then back up. "You know eventually you will have to marry me."

His lips lifted in a small grin. "Oh, I plan to, darlin'. I didn't want to ask without a ring and doin' it up proper."

"Will you make love to me now?"

"Right now?"

"Yeah. I've missed having you surround me."

"It would be my pleasure, darlin'."

She didn't waste any time getting her clothes off so she could feel him, the friction of his skin against hers, the rough rub of the hair on his body over the softer surface of her own, and the ridges of his muscles as she ran her hands over his chest.

He lifted her in his arms, carrying her to the big bed in the corner before laying her down on the wedding-ring quilt. It seemed fitting now.

His clothes fell away from his body as he stripped down to nothing. She'd almost forgotten how magnificent he was to look at, to touch, and to love.

She raised her arms, welcoming him into her embrace.

When his skin finally touched hers, she sighed. She'd come home.

Epilogue

Joseph spread the quilt out on the sand near the pond. The late summer evening seemed the perfect time. They'd been together for several months now and he realized every day how much he loved Rose and wanted her in his life. It had seemed strange at first, how she'd become such a part of him when he hadn't been looking for love at all.

She'd given up her life in New York and moved to Bandera right after the water incident. He'd even gone to New York with her to help her move her stuff. That had been an adventure and a half since he'd never been there. Life there seemed way too fast for a cowboy like him.

"Joseph?" She held out her hand after she placed the picnic basket on the quilt, guiding him to her side. "Are you hungry?"

"I'm starving."

She laughed. "Aren't you always?"

"Probably." He sank down on the quilt as she took out the chicken, potato salad, bottle of wine, and dessert from the basket. "Did you cook this?"

"Yes, sir. I've been taking lessons in Southern cooking from the women in the kitchen."

"It looks great, Rose."

She handed him a plate, holding it back so she could kiss him before he took it. The little sneaky grin on her lips made him wonder what she might be up to. He was the one with the surprise.

They talked during the meal about several things including the ranch, the fantastic number of guests they'd had this year, how the horses were doing in the heat of the summer, and her latest project at her job.

She'd been hired as a research microbiologist for a large lab in San Antonio at a really good salary. "It's a great project. I can't go into details, but I think the outcome will be something very important to the development of some new drugs."

"As long as you enjoy what you're doin', nothing else matters."

"Oh, I do. I'm excited to see where this all goes."

She slid the fork between her lips, making him think about those lips around his cock. Had it only been this morning since they'd made love? He couldn't seem to get enough of her.

"Stop looking at me like that, Joseph."

"Like what?"

"Like you want to eat me alive."

"I do." He set his plate down and crawled toward her. "You have no idea how much I want you."

"Here?"

"Yep. It was one of the first places we made love after we met. Seems kind of fitting, don't you think?"

She glanced around as a smile spread across her lips.

He leaned in and kissed her softly on the lips. He wanted to do something before they made love again. This time they would be bound together for the rest of their lives. "Rose?" He sat back on his heels, taking her hand in his.

A frown turned down the corners of her mouth. "Yes?"

"I need to ask you somethin'. It's important, so if you want to take some time to think about it, that's okay." He reached into the front pocket of his jeans. "I love you with all my heart. You've become the most important thing in my life. I know you've given up a ton to be here with me in Texas, and you have no idea how much that means to me." She gasped as he opened the small box in his hands. "Will you marry me?"

"Oh, Joseph," she whispered. "Of course, I'll marry you. I love you."

He took out the ring he'd spent the last few months saving for and slid it onto her left ring finger. "From my heart and soul this cowboy's promise is to love you forever."

She launched herself into his arms and they fell back against the quilt, laughing. She pelted him with kisses all over his face until she finally reached his mouth. When she paused, he looked up into her gorgeous green eyes and saw what he'd always wanted but never realized it until he'd found it.

Love.

The End

About the Author

Sandy Sullivan is a romance author, who, when not writing, spends her time with her husband Shaun on their farm in middle Tennessee. She loves to ride her horses, play with their dogs and relax on the porch, enjoying the rolling hills of her home south of Nashville. Country music is a passion of hers and she loves to listen to it while she writes.

She is an avid reader of romance novels and enjoys reading Nora Roberts, Jude Deveraux and Susan Wiggs. Finding new authors and delving into something different helps feed the need for literature. A registered nurse by education, she loves to help people and spread the enjoyment of romance to those around her with her novels. She loves cowboys so you'll find many of her novels have sexy men in tight jeans and cowboy boots.

Sandy's website
www.romancestorytime.com

Other books by Sandy

Love Me Once, Love Me Twice (Montana Cowboys 1)
Before the Night is Over (Montana Cowboys 2)
Two for the Price of One (Montana Cowboys 3)
Difficult Choices (Montana Cowboys 4)
Doctor Me Up (Montana Cowboys 5)
Stakin' His Claim
Country Minded Cougar
Meet Me in the Barn
Taming the Cougar
Trouble With a Cowboy
Gotta Love a Cowboy
Make Mine a Cowboy (Cowboy Dreamin' 1)
Healing a Cowboy's Heart (Cowboy Dreamin' 2)
For the Love of a Cowboy (Cowboy Dreamin' 3)
Tempted by the Cowboy (Cowboy Dreamin' 4)
Forever Kind of Cowboy (Cowboy Dreamin' 5)
Kiss Me, Cowboy (Cowboy Dreamin' 6)
A Cowboy and a Country Song (Cowboy Dreamin' 7)
A Cowboy of My Own (Cowboy Dreamin' 8)
Falling Hard (Eight Second Ride Book 1)
Loving Hard (Eight Second Ride Book 2)